EMOTIONAL ROLLERCOASTER

BY

Emma Cruize

CONTENTS

WOEBEGONE

W ell, where do I start? I'm just a normal woman really, You'd not pay me much attention if I walked past you in the street, but I have a past I'm choosing to share, A story to tell, I've realised I can dwell on my past or use it to help others I am choosing to put my bad past to a good future (hopefully) and attempt to write a book, my English teacher once said I would so why heck not can't be that hard right? (Mr Blackburn you was right after all) Well to start with I am 37 years old (younger in my mind) with a body of a 70 odd-year-old!

Not how for a minute I ever thought I'd be in my 30's. I was raised in the UK in a town called Doncaster to a not so well off troubled home life, my mother is Narcissistic and all I've ever known is trouble and strife. Forced to marry at 16 and the abuse continued on ranging from mental and physical to sexual and what can only be described as torture at times, from a very young age until I turned 27 years old, first at the hands of my mum then after a few years it was her 'lodger/friend' my ex-husband, Government agencies from NHS to Education just to name a few whom have let me down over the years one way, shape or form. This is the story of my life, the good, the bad and the plain ugly, a lot of emotion and tears have gone into writing this and I hope it shows how cruel life can be but also how YOU can change that and become happier and satisfied in life as I now am.
Only a very short while ago I had everything or so It seemed, I will explain further into the book but for now, let me tell you

nothing is ever as it seems! From the outside view it would seem I had everything, I mean I had 4 wonderful children, a not so great husband who was an idiot but he knew oh too well how to hide that extremely well to others, and what seemed to be in everyone's eyes a great life so everyone told me by telling me how very lucky I was and how I should be grateful for what I have not what I don't have! I had a 3-bed house with lovely big garden, a 14ft touring caravan and a modern car the idyllic lifestyle really If only people knew the truth as nothing is ever black and white.

The reality of my life was extremely different though, you see I was a teen mum and not all was as picture-perfect as it first appeared, let me explain further this is a long read of my life and will explain who I am and why I am today writing this, my life really is a rollercoaster ride of emotions and I am choosing to share it with you! There are a number of stops on this roller-coaster ranging from sheer happiness, love and fun to pain and heartache and tears aplenty from mental torture to abuse both mentally and physically! I hope with this book it will assist those going through or have suffered abuse, anxiety & depression which sadly we all suffer from at one point in our lives or another. I cannot guarantee this book will cure you but do hope it shows there is light at end of the tunnel as you'll see by the ending and hope it teaches you that with positive thinking and future goals and facing the problems you can have that happy ending.

I'd like to thank my husband and friends for supporting me through this book to my husband especially for holding me in your arms throughout the bad times and never letting me down and showing me what true/real love is, I am dedicating this to you all who have supported me over the years and to each and every one of you who reads it. Thank you!

Feel free to join my Facebook page:
@Emma Cruize Emotional Rollercoaster

MY EARLY CHILDHOOD IN MY EYES, THE GOOD YEARS!

I was born in Doncaster Royal Infirmary on the 17th Sep 1982, I was born with a condition some babies suffer with called jaundice which basically made my skin yellow looking and I had to be put into an incubator for a short while, I had jet black hair and was a little chubby baby at 8lb 8oz with blue eyes, well compared to how I am now anyhow, not that I weigh less now of cause! I remember my mum telling me that she was gutted at missing top of the pops which was on at the time of me deciding now was the time to arrive I love music now I guess that explains things huh!

Obviously, I don't really remember much until I was maybe 3 years old roughly but I have been told that my mum, my nanna whose name is Ruby Leggs who I can only describe as a very kind, loving person with a smart appearance and my Uncle Edward whom was nothing more than a total fruit bat, he had such a warm addictive personality always got a story to tell and a sense of humour that made him shine brightly and the brightest blue eye's I'd ever seen, Yes I truly admired and looked up to my Uncle dearly, They both played a HUGE part in my childhood and into my later adult life too. I lived with my mum Jossalynn in a little village called Stanford which was roughly 7 miles from the town called Doncaster in South Yorkshire, UK, My mum is called Jossalynn she had me at 21 years old, everyone used to tell me I were her double growing up, all my life we have always had the nickname of double trouble, and people often told me you two are cloned as by time I was 2 my hair started turning blonde same as my mum's and we had the same facial features which I can only describe as average looking, oval face, high cheek bones and both wore glasses, nothing overly special really. For the first maybe 5 or 6 years or so of my life, we were close, extremely close and I will always remember those years I just wish things were still that way.

I remember the earliest story about my life I were told by my nanna and then my mum some years later as I was growing up was that my uncle Edward and his friend nidge I think his name was would take me to the youth club in Stanford to play cricket! Nothing wrong with that though right, I mean sport is good for children apart from I was only at that time no more than a couple of months old. I was also told and slightly recall that my nanna would also collect me from my mum's quite often especially on a foggy or rainy day as she loved walking in the that type of weather and would take me with her in my pushchair as she went on her long walks chatting to me while we went across the bridge into the next village to the supermarket at Duncraft or to were ever she used to need to go it really didn't matter for one I was too young to raise much a concern I could barely say a sentence at the age I would've been at this point, never mind protest at anything hahaha, I loved spending time with my nanna even at such a young age I remember feeling too close to her and very much loved, It's a memory I will always treasure so very much.

My first years As I grew into a toddler I idolised my mum possibly looking back way too much though at the time I never realised this, At the time I hold many memories were I recall that I wanted to be just like her when I grew up (what was I thinking exactly?), As I remember it though we were sooo very close until I turned 3ish? Every evening my mum would get me ready for bed you know the usual routine, bath, nightwear on, supper and then my favourite time where we would both cuddle up, Laid down together on the sofa just my mum and I on our big brown sofa it was our special time and we would watch TV together until I would fall asleep and my mum would always leave me their until she herself went to bed at which point she would then carry me upstairs to my bed not that I often stayed in my own bed at this age.

At around 3 years old maybe younger I threatened to leave home, I packed a little bag which contained my dolly Sarah and few other items of which I do not recall what they were but I do know that it wasn't anything of use, I did this because I was constantly being told off by my mum, I don't obviously recall what for half the time it was for nothing but I remember being shouted at and feeling frightened a lot and on this occasion I decided I wanted to go and live with my nanna, I remember feeling so angry and upset and I was in tears sobbing my little heart out and quite possibly the first time I felt anger I just couldn't calm down I was so hurt and so fed up of my mummy being mean to me and I not knowing why, so off I went I only got to end of the street before I ran back to my mum who was stood at the gate yelling down the street in a cheery voice to tell nanna that mummy would be round in morning to make sure I am ok and she said goodbye and waved to me, I guess I was scared to leave or the long distance I had to go ,maybe it was just that I didn't really deep down want to leave my mummy or home, who really knows as I certainly do not remember why but I ran back and was told to get back in the house and upon doing so I was told how daft I was and told I was a coward, weak and would never amount to anything if I could not even make it to my nanna's what hope did I have, she laughed and told me to get to my room and not to dare try and challenge her again at least until I was much more grown up and stood a chance as I obviously needed her and I realised there and then my mummy was right, I did need her, I was little, everything was big, I was stupid and daft and a coward and wouldn't survive without my mum, No I had to try harder to be a good girl that'd make my mummy happier.

I didn't understand any of her words to be honest apart from they was not things to be proud or happy about and I must remember them, learn them and try hard not to be those words but they haunt my dreams and memories even today and affected me in my childhood badly in many ways but especially in my confidence.

I hold a lot of different memories around this time but still as of yet my childhood is patchy what I recall and don't is varied, there are huge gaps of time's as of yet I for whatever reason there's many months or possibly even years that I don't recall at all very well I can only presume my memory has still blocked much of the bad out, I do recall after this incident that life continued to improve slightly, though I don't know why nor really cared all that mattered was that my mum was happier which meant I got yelled at less and was happier too and I remember us moving to a house on Large Square, Stanford this is the very first home I remember properly it was on a little square I could play out on safely and best thing is my nanna only lived at bottom of the square and often came up to ours or us to visit my nanna, we remained here for a good few years I was about 4 years old at the time and remember all the children played on the square and I their met what would become my best friend in childhood Rachel Shaw amongst other children of same and older age, I liked it there and felt happy and made many friends, it was their I also discovered I had a special talent but at this age I just thought everyone had it, the house was a typical 1980s council house in a mining village it had 3 bedrooms (my mums, mine and a toy room) and bathroom upstairs and Livingroom and kitchen downstairs with a front garden that led onto the square and a back door that led onto the backings I knew I wasn't allowed to use this door ever, Anyhow one evening I woke up as I heard voices well giggling, I sat up in bed it was dark, reached for my glasses put them on and listened I didn't feel scared more curious who were the children? I crept out of my bed and walked towards the giggling.....What I saw next I have never forgot, Their I stood silently frozen to spot in my toy room doorway I stood and their totally unaware I was there was a girl and a boy but they was see through almost and my teddies was what looked like floating.... That was it I ran screaming to my mum and a panic attack brought on a very bad asthma attack I was 3ish years old I remember running my mum grabbing me then next thing I recall was a bright light, I went towards it and all a sudden was a beautiful scene I wasn't sure if I was dreaming or what but I knew I had to go closer, look more, I wanted to go on that grass but there was huge gates and everyone was behind them, There was a sign with names and dates upon it and I saw mine wasn't their then this voice asked my name I replied Emma Ward and he said no you're not on list turn around go back, I said like a typical 3 year old one simple thing " Why?" to which I was simply told it is not your time, You have a very important job to do, again I asked what and how would I know? I didn't get any answers I suddenly was looking down at my body, I was in hospital, Dr's and nurses and machines bleeping around me a silly mask on my mouth and nose and I could hear my mum crying and saying Emma get back in your body please and then I saw my mum looking up at me, I looked around and the Nurses and Dr's was looking at my mum sadly and saying something about time of death I suddenly opened my eyes and was looking up at my mum for around a second before she grabbed me sobbing and the nurse a dark skinned lady just walked over sat down and started asking me questions one I recall was what did I just see? I explained all I have just written here and I recall the nurse

11

turning to my mum and saying your daughter died, she had an amazing experience it's called a near death experience or something like that but she then asked me to describe the man who told me to go back, upon doing so which was long dark hair, slim man, beard with a dress I said as i laughed at a man in a dress to which she ran yes ran off out the room and quickly returned with a yellow book and asked me if the person was in this I flicked the pages and stopped and said YES this that him, that IS him ... why who is the man?

The nurse and my mum was looking at each other jaws wide open and the nurse simply said that is Jesus I thought oh ok and fell asleep, I mean I didn't know at the time who he was. After this at home more strange things happened, etc. one time I was on sofa in living room and my mum on floor making the fire, In walked my nanna and as she entered the Livingroom a black shadowy figure flew past her really fast and my nanna just looked horrified, not much was said but my nanna visited less and talk of a new home was mentioned.

TOO YOUNG TO BE LEFT!

A few months maybe a year or so after this we moved when I was about 5 years old to another house still in Stainford this is when the very first of my abuse/bad memories really started...... All of a sudden life change dramatically my mum started making new friends one I was introduced to as my Aunt Scarlet and her two daughters, welcome to the first stop on what I call my emotional rollercoaster ride, not that it was like that all the time we still had more good days than bad, sure there were times when I felt life could be better one for example was when my mum started going out to the pub's on a weekend mostly Friday or Saturday nights with my Aunt Scarlet and left her eldest daughter to babysit me, I hated those time's I don't recall them much as I tried to block them out but the bad memories don't go do they so easily all I remember is been told to shut up and go my room all the time by my aunt Scarlet's daughters, even if I wanted toilet which was downstairs just outside the backdoor in an outside area or a drink from the kitchen or just simply couldn't sleep etc., I would get yelled at, get called a baby and told to go back upstairs out there way and to leave them alone as they don't like me and don't wish to see me or they'd tell my mum I'd been naughty and I would be in serious trouble, I knew how my mum could be, she scared me so I ran up to my room and their I stayed until morning! My mum was not aware of this I mean she raved on and on about how great Scarlet was and how great her daughter was for looking after me but Scarlet's daughter who was only a teenager herself as I explained had already told me if I told my mum she would not believe me as they would inform her that I was lying so what was the point in me trying? Half the time my mum never believed a word I said I didn't feel happy or loved but extremely confused, lost and frightened.

STARTING SCHOOL!

I remember my first teacher Mrs Thompson at 5 or so years old, wow what a teacher! She was amazing, kind generous and very good at her job she had me reading and writing very quickly not bad for a 5-year-old! I remember only a few months after me starting school my mum started helping out voluntary at the school I attended which was at that time Stanford Infant School there was no such thing as a Primary school back in the mid-'80s at first my mum was a voluntary classroom assistant this is where she met more friends, My mum's 'job' was listening to the other children read for an hour or 2 per day and then later maybe a year or 2 when I was around 6/7 years old she also became a dinner lady so I always saw her.

This was wonderful I got extra pudding and custard oh how I loved that especially when it was chocolate concrete and strawberry custard YUM! Life really was quite enjoyable most the time since I had started school apart from the weekends when my mum went to the pub still and I was extremely happy especially when my mum stopped going out as much a few months after, I felt very much loved once again as a child should do, back to just my mum and I again things seemed perfect. My dad was not around as a child or ever in my life, my mum was having an affair with a married man and I am the result of that and obviously, the man didn't wish to know once my mum decided to keep the baby, I do remember when my mum first met Billy her on/ off fiancé (more off than on) he was the only Dad

I've ever known. I remember one time me and my mum were walking down the street in Stanford the village we then lived on our way to the carboot as we did every Sunday and my mum suddenly stopped and pointed to this man in across the street and said that man there with the brown curly/wavy hair and cream coat, Yes I replied.. well he is your dad, I remember him clearly even though I was very young at the time, he was tall, thin and had long hair his name my mum informed me was Mitch, I shouted dad to which he looked at me and said I'm no dad of yours, it was at that point I decided ok this man is not worthy to be called dad, but Billy was different he always called me his little princess and would treat me as his own I think I was the closest he's ever come to having children, though I am not entirely sure if he ever went on to have any children of his own, I don't really recall Billy coming into our life's all I remember is one day there were me and my mum and she was happier and not going out and those horrible girls of Aunt Scarlets was no longer around then the next Billy was just there like he'd never not been coming to our home for meals after his long hard work as a miner down local pit. Billy would often take me swimming in our local town in Doncaster a bus ride away, I loved going on the bus we often didn't do so, He was teaching me to swim, supporting my stomach and gliding me through the water I thought I was brilliant that I was swimming all alone I had very little confidence even at such a young age but around Billy, I felt I had loads afterwards we would go to McDonalds I loved those days. I remember my mum and Billy had some very bad arguments, Though I do not recall what about I just remember the loud voices than the quiet as I walked into the room, one time Billy told my mum it was not right to argue in front of me and they should talk about things calmly, this I am guessing was a huge mistake as not long after maybe a week or so Billy came to visit he'd not been around since that day, I was about 7 years old may be at the time and I remember my mum making Billy's tea I was happy life was back to normal I'd missed Billy and swimming, he did not live with us but i wished he did my mum was nicer to me when he was around. Well on this day I saw my mum making a pie (my mum never baked apart from Christmas) She had just rolled the pastry and layer it into a pie dish and was just opening a tin of dog food nothing peculiar about that right we had 2 Alsatian dogs so quite perfectly normal that she should be feeding them right before sorting the pie filling? Wrong... She was opening the tin to put the contents in Billy's pie as the filling..... Yes, you read that right! The reason behind this was Billy was a miner and my mum was annoyed that he was part of the miners' strike at Hatfield Colliery, Stanford and because of that and him at the time not supporting her financially at the time she made him a dog meat pie, the poor guy ate it and commented on how nice it was and said it was the best pie he'd ever tasted! Yuk my mum then went on to tell Billy what he had just ate and to tell him he was sleeping with the dogs that night in a kennel outside! Charming! The poor guy actually did just that in the pouring rain in the middle of winter; I know you're probably thinking why did he put up with such abuse? Well Billy was in love with my mum he adored her, He worshipped the ground she walked on and he would've done anything to keep her happy.

That was really the very last I remember of him the next morning my mum took me school kicked his feet he came out the kennel she said go home before someone sees you ya daft idiot and when I came home he wasn't their nor did he ever come around or I see him again, I missed him so very much but whenever I mentioned Billy to my mum to enquire where he was etc. she always got angry with me and told me I'd not understand, he wasn't my dad, it didn't matter so leave it alone, he may not have been my real dad and I may not have called him so but he was like my dad and I felt confused and upset but also felt I could not express my feelings to anyone as I wasn't really seeing anyone apart from teachers and my mum at this time i wasn't allowed outside or least i don't think i ever was as i never recall doing so in back garden we had 2 big Alsatians so i never went out alone so i don't remember much fun around this time at all i lived for school, loved school, this time was the start of a very slippery slope that was until recently the story of my life, not a good way for a 7-year-old to feel huh?

The first really bad memories I have started when I was around maybe 6 or 7 years old possibly when my depression first started and my confidence totally failed me as I don't really recall being happy with my mum at all around this time of my life at home with her sadly apart from odd time, With Billy out our life's for some reason my mum started going out with her friend Scarlet again leaving me with these 2 strangers I was told they were my cousins, Liz and Peaches who used to watch me only a little while back but I had not had anything to do with since then even though they were my mum's 'new' best friend's daughters who i was expected to suddenly be best friends with and like!

Liz was the same age as me and I did not get along with her what so ever, Peaches was older, she was the one my mum instructed I listen to and was to look after me while she went to the pub with their mother whom I was told was my aunt Scarlet all I remember of Aunt Scarlet is that she had dark curly hair and wore very big thick glasses.

Now I know it's no big deal everyone leaves their kids to go out-right, parents deserve a break? But have you ever thought about the consequences of this on a child's mental wellbeing? I'll tell you how I felt, I felt with-drawn upset and worried, Change no matter how little without proper explanation affects us all no matter of the age don't you agree?

Well, let's say this became a regular occurrence every Friday and Saturday night my mum and Scarlet would yet again go out to the local pubs to get hammered let it be the New Inn or one in

FishLake or Askern or often a pub crawl which is when you start at one destination agree upon a final destination and hit every pub in-between with goal of reaching final pub stood upright and able to get served or least that's what my mum informed me her and my Aunt did on a night out when i asked once and once again I was left at home, left to tuck myself into bed, no one to talk to as the so-called babysitter was horrible still to me, she'd not changed at all and never even spoke to me only to yet again just like last time tell me to shut up and go to my room, never mind cared for me, basically I was left to tend to my own needs from 7 years old to around 8 or so years old!

I felt miserable what young child should be made to feel like that? My school work started suffering it felt like my mum wasn't my mum any more, the only way I can explain is I felt isolated, scared and confused and very upset, I didn't understand why my mum wasn't making a huge fuss of me like she used too when Billy was around, I felt pushed away emotionally and physically and I started spending more time with my Nanna who is called Ruby Leggs.

My nanna was and still is a blast, good fun and very loving and extremely caring with a heart of gold her youthful looks (she's in her mid-80's now but does not look a day past 65) and brilliant mannerism she really was and still is the most amazing person I've ever known I only hope I can be half the woman she is, she at this time in book has black hair that is when she was outside always worn in a head scarf but inside was classic 1980s military wife style, smart, tidy and very elegant looking, her dress style was the same apart from always seemed to have a pinny on back then and smelt of cigarette smoke, I never really did like that smell as a child, my mum didn't smoke so I wasn't around it often.

I don't really recall much from the time after I left Mrs Thompsons class at school strangely at home or school at all, I recall going school, coming home, but I don't hold no memories of birthdays or any Christmases or any day trips or any other significant childhood memories happening at all, What I do recall is the daft times that I found quite fun for example the one memory I have right now is there was a knock at the front door and my mum laughing and saying quick time to play the game Emz, I remember me and my mum laying down snuggled up behind the sofa hidden from window and the number one rule of the game being we cannot EVER let the person see us or hear us we must be still, well-hidden and super quiet and I would win if he walked away, I thought these times was so fun as it was only time my mum played with me, I'd try hard not to giggle knowing if I kept extra still and extra quiet as she told me, like the rules was til she said the safe word which was 'Super Spaz' upon my mum saying this we had to jump up in a super hero pose and shout loudly 'Super Spaz' together for winning my prize was always a cuddle and a treat!

I later found out this was either the TV licence man, Loan man or the other idiots as they was later described to me when I later asked as an adult who they were back then she said Social Services I also obviously learnt later in life that the word Spaz that my mum learnt me and thought was such a great game was not a nice word at all and now that word totally repulses me beyond belief!

Not long after these times I recall suddenly clearer memories and happier times as I was I think 'living' unofficially with my nanna though as of yet no one has ever fully explained this time I spent with my nanna to me so it's really hazy I mean try to imagine it one moment I'm at home with my mum living in Stanford near the school and fairly unhappy, I go to school and next in my memories I'm living with my nanna she collected me from school one evening and informs me I will be sleeping at her for a little while, I didn't even ask why I was just too excited and could not wait to do so, I sort of moved in to her house again back on small Square in Stanford but having to share a bed with her, but she was being a mum to me, this still is confusing as what did happen? Why I was suddenly with my nanna was all time and NEVER saw my mum at all?

I'll explain what I recall to best I can; my nanna would take me to school each morning as I was now sleeping at hers every evening in fact at this time I do not recall going home or even seeing my mum at all, I now went to the village middle school and on the way their each morning we would walk to the local shop called Pippins and I remember my nanna treating me to a packet of crisps and sometimes even a chocolate bar for the break time and she would see me to the school gates whilst chatting away to me and laughing together, she would also be the one to collect me from school and cook my tea, omg I absolutely loved my nanna's cooking especially one meal she called corned beef hash and the way she would put me in my place should I need it, though more often than not I listened, my nanna is strict and you soon learned it was best to be on her good side rather than not.

Life continued like this for a while I can't remember my exact age but I think i was around 8 or 9 yrs. old and it was roughly between 1989 to 1992'ish that I spent this time with my nanna, but there was many a good times in this period of my life, I was able to hang out with my mates after school too, something I had previously never been able to do since leaving Small Square, it was sheer bliss.

I recall I had plenty of friends at this time, Maisy Waxfield, Rachel Chow, Kelly, Faye, Sarah, Craig, Ben, Lil Craig it was a village where everyone knew everyone and was a real community spirit and all us kids was friends with each other and never did seem to be any fighting or bullying on scale we see today and people watched out for each other's children so we was safe to hang out around the whole village as back then it really was safe to do so!

I really enjoyed life in these years but I still to this day do not know why it changed or even why I ended up with my nanna from roughly 1989-1992'ish that is a really approximate guess in the years as I honestly am not sure how many years I was with my nanna or the exact age I was when I first went to live with my nanna but I recall I was in last year of infant school when I last at this point remember seeing my mum and then next thing I remember is being with my nanna, attending Junior school and being extremely happy but feeling like I had been there forever it felt normal?

After a birthday party one evening I think I was around 10'ish whilst I was at my nannas to be honest I do not recall one time my mum ever threw me a birthday party or overly celebrated my birthday anyhow this one time I recall my nanna talking about my mum and how I'd not seen her, I asked why she had not even attended my party but all I got was that she'd done something stupid and that she had put my dad's wife Jane Freeman through the butcher window when she called me a specky four eyed bitch, my nanna then went on to say I would be seeing my mum more now very soon and everything would go back to how it was, I just remember being confused thinking what was normal?

I only recalled being happy with my nanna, I honestly didn't want it to change, the next memory I remember I was back with my mum and travelling to school on bus each day like nothing had ever happened, it was so strange, I tried to speak of this time and ask questions to my mum often but she would just tell me to please leave it, or tell me not now love. I soon learnt was no point in me asking my mum for answers. I felt really confused, started missing my nanna as I was no longer even seeing her and felt quite down, life wasn't bad just I felt down and did not understand a lot of things which caused mass confusion, I started to hate silence as when was quiet my mind would have all these questions running through it and I soon learnt how to block them out by being busy nonstop, mentally or physically this really did seem to help at the time.

One of my favourite memories not long after this period was of one of the school 6 week summer holidays I remember them well, my mum & me, my aunty Jossalynn and her two daughters Michelle & Raven and my best friend at the time Rachel and the very best part of all was that my nanna was coming along too i hardly ever saw her since returning back to my mum which hurt a lot as I missed my nanna soo very much indeed but I was told it was now Candies (my nannas now second eldest Granddaughter who was my Aunt Mary first born) It was now Candy turn to now sleep at my nannas and I had to stop being nasty and share my nanna now and grow up, so I thought nothing more of it even though I was obviously hurt and felt pushed away.

Anyhow back to the holiday we always went to a place called Cleethorpes on the East Coast Uk, We went there every year it was a sort of Yorkshire holiday hotspot, back then it used to be fun (very different to how it is today in 2019 no offence at all intended but it really has changed) the holidays were great, well mostly apart from the one year when my nanna didn't go, I felt I had my mum back again away from Stanford and that horrible Scarlet and her other friends, awesome times, just wish they lasted!

WHAT HAPPENS IN CLEETHORPESSTAYS IN CLEETHORPES!

S adly one of the following years though my nanna didn't come on holiday and that ruined it big style for me, this year there was only me, my mum, my Aunt Jossalynn and her 2 daughters Raven who was a few years older than me maybe early teens she was tall and very slim with shoulder length purple hair that she always wore tied back in a high pony tail and always wore black even in hottest weather and was never happy, always moody and angry looking and Michelle she was 1 year older than me she was exact opposite of her sister, she had natural looks with her wavy mousey brown hair and was a little on big side and always wore bright colours and normally cheerful, We always went on the train our parents moaning about how heavy cases was, if to catch bus, walk or get taxi to the caravan site from the train station and often getting into a right old state then suddenly laughing often leaving us kids really confused, Upon arrival this time we caught the open topped bus to the caravan site and checked in at Beachcomber and found our chalet, We hadn't even unpacked when my mum declared wanted to go to shops and post office before it closed and off we set, I was only young this holiday memory I'd say 9 or 10 ish and seemed to be ages we had been walking and then we was at a place i knew not far from shop and she told me to wait with Raven and Michelle on the boating lake park and sandpit and go nowhere else and do as they said or else!

I resented and put up such a fuss to try make my mum take me with her but my mum just got firm and shouted at me which made me mad and upset and feeling very scared too, she informed me again in a more stern tone and her usual I am not messing around look she had more a glare really her eye's bore through me at these times. Icy cold almost careless and evil they scared me more than her voice, She told me to stay with them both and we were to stay on the boating lake and not move far, As soon as my mum and aunt Jossalynn were out of eye sight Raven turned to Michelle smiled and said ready and stated telling me 'we are going for a walk' I told them 'no way we are to stay here, You know my mum said we were not to leave this area or else', Raven then shouted at me and told me I was to go with them or they'd leave me here all alone see how big I was then for not listening to her and see how much trouble I would be in!

I was a young child and looked even younger than my age too!! I started crying and Raven called me a baby, laughed told Michelle to come on and off they both went laughing, leaving me stood in middle of the boating lake car park with cars and coaches coming and going around me during the high season first week in August, I stood their frozen to spot my mum had left me only minutes earlier but now very much out of my sight given how tiny I was back then and was over a duel carriage way so I knew I could not safely cross that alone, I started panicking, I was not brave, I was scared, I was crying and alone and extremely scared, this man saw me crying and approached me, I think he was with his family at the time but he came over alone, I was scared this was a stranger, someone, I didn't know but I was more scared of being alone so when he put his hand on my shoulder and asked if I were ok I spoke to him and told him no I was not ok and explained about how my cousins had left me, he then asked were my mum & dad were, my mum then suddenly appeared and acted all shocked and horrified at me crying and she thanked the man and pulled me close telling me it was ok and not to run off in future and the man said something about kids then walked off but as soon as he had left my mum called me a stupid, stupid silly little girl and told me I should have stayed with Raven and I'd spoiled there sneaky drink in the pub and how she hoped I was happy and wasn't hoping to do anything for rest of day as I wasn't going to now!

The rest of the holiday I recall being mostly in pubs, One memory was my mum and Aunt Jossalynn was both quite tipsy if not drunk and was stood laughing at the bar us kids could see them from the children's room where we was told to stay put and behave and play nicely, I was not really one to mix with people easily so I stood awkwardly just looking at my mum and wishing I was having as much fun, I sat on a step and recall a man going up to her and talking and them all laughing so much and the song Achy Breaky Heart on the radio, My mum then saw me and waved me over and was acting strangely all a sudden all loving and affectionate kissing me on my head, hugging me close to her I honestly did not care why she was acting this was I was very happy and I showed it I hugged her tightly back and told her I love you mummy you're the best and I ran off happy back in the play area.

That is all I remember of that holiday! We didn't really go on many more holidays after that one I am pleased to say.

Upon coming home from that holiday my mum talked of us moving to a flat in Doncaster she had found us while I was staying with nanna those few years, the estate as my mum described it to me (she never took me to view home until she'd actually moved in by time I first saw it she'd settled in and lived there by looks of it a while but I knew the estate from times we had passed it on way to visit my Aunt the occasional times on the bus, It had 3 main roads around it, was very close to town and has a mixture of homes on it, a council housing estate mostly with houses, multiple blocks of 3 story flats, high rise flats, old folks centre a school and few shops and a park, It wasn't anything special nor was it anything bad either, I liked the sound and look of it, I was both excited and upset at thought though at same time, upset I was told I could no longer stay at my nannas and excited at seeing and being home with my mum, finding out why she'd gone, and where too, why she had missed my birthday etc.

A NEW TOWN

We moved into one of the high raised flat's on a estate known as Balby Bridge Flats in Doncaster well I say we but my mum had clearly lived here a while before I was allowed to move in as it was decorated, fully furnished with all new stuff not one item from our old life's was anywhere to be seen, all my old items gone, I asked where all was and was told we have new and do not need old so do not worry about that, I wasn't worried I just found it rather strange, there was no evidence that showed my mum had just moved in as everyone was telling me, she knew everyone, it seemed she had definitely lived here a few months!

The block of flats we moved into was called Sandbeck house our home was on the 8th floor and my Uncle Edward my mums twin brother lived on the 12th floor of the same block of flats which was pretty cool with his wife and for a short while his wife's son and my mum also had gotten friends with this guy our next-door neighbour Larry Lambert, he was gay and so much fun to be around, I loved the fact that my mum had a friend that saw us as 2 separate people as most my mum's 'other' friends never even acknowledged my existence and often just pretended I wasn't around or made me feel unwanted etc. but Larry showed me he wanted me around, he treated me as an equal even though I was only under 10ish or at least i found out what gay was and that Larry was Gay once my mum and Larry sat me down and explained instead of girls liking boys Larry was different as some people are in life and went on to make it perfectly clear that this is perfectly fine and shouldn't be looked ever as a bad thing as some might tell me as they are the bad people who say it's bad as it's not, I asked what wasn't bad to which my mum went on to explain that Larry liked other men not women so with that explanation at that time i felt at the time I was quite mature and understood what gay meant fully and felt quite mature that they'd sat explained something important to me, I remember Larry well, He was very camp, funny, kind to me and knew a lot of famous people off the TV, I remember going out to school one day as I was still in school in village i used to live in with my nanna and my mum took us to school on the bus each morning, anyhow on this morning I remember seeing a band member from a very famous band that everyone knows from the late '80s/ 90's era stood there in the communal corridor!

He asked if I knew who he was when I said yes and he laughed said he was going to Larry's nice to meet me and asked my name! Larry threw some amazing parties I remember one time at Halloween he threw a party where there were quite a few people from TV i knew faces off amongst others, I was nervous at first but Larry soon made me feel relaxed he had apple bobbing, music, lights, food and everything I loved it but the memory that stuck in my mind is Larry going down to his bedroom and reappearing dressed in these tight little black leather shorts with fairy light's draped all over him and angel wings and a wand in his hand and said well hello big boys your resident fairy is here, I recall quite a few of these famous people telling Larry off saying she's too young this is not right and save it for later, Larry was quite tipsy and said omg I am so sorry I didn't think at all, but my mum just laughed and said it is fine she is mature and seen far worse.... Had I? And if so what cause I aint sure I certainly don't recall what and at the party everyone was looking at my mum with this strange look on their faces and she turned said to Larry right I had better get Emma ready for bed, Come on

Emz we are off and I thanked Larry, Gave everyone a cuddle and left and went next door and to bed.

Even though Larry was gay he started asking my mum out, saying he adored me and wanted us all to be a proper family and would love to adopt me and make me his daughter, obviously she refused but he kept on over the following weeks, he asked my mum to marry him and eventually they drifted apart and their friendship ended.

Things for a short while were still great at the flat though I wasn't seeing Larry as much, me & my mum shared many silly times together etc. one hot summer day we filled up water balloons and threw them over the balcony from the 8th floor I remember 1 of the water bombs hitting a poor man on the head I couldn't help but laugh and my mum was also in stitches, even though it is quite cruel the poor man looked up horrified then started waving his stick up at us telling us this won't be the last we'd hear of this, I remember me and my mum running back into the flat laughing sooo very much and saying how funny that was but we'd better not do it any more as we would get into trouble.

I never did get around to asking my mum all the questions about where she had gone all that time, why I never saw her etc. I did try but she said it didn't matter as it was the past and my mum's motto is the past is past, tomorrow is a new day so forget the past and live for today only! I was told this each and every time, I can't stand any phrase similar now, I still have those questions as an adult now and doubt they shall ever be answered.

Another memory I have is my mum starting to once again begin to act quite strangely, her behaviour slowly changing becoming more moody, distant and quieter then next moment loud and boisterous it was really confusing. One strong memory I have around this time give or take a few months maybe was while I was in Junior School not long after returning back to my mum we was at bus stop waiting for the bus like we did each evening after school and was always so busy, my mum randomly just started tickling me i laughed so much and almost cried before she stopped, Next day she tickled me more I had to beg her to stop I recall saying "Mum please stop it really hurts, please mummy, I love you it hurts" and crying, she laughed said awww toughen up, I'm only playing with you ya daft bugger and hugged me close, over those next couple weeks it got steadily worse and she started the 'play fights' with me, Yes it hurt when she punched me and I often said ouch/ cried but she said she was messing and only playing, plus it wasn't really that hard I guess, then called me a little bitch, I thought this is how mum's treat their children and this is how we were meant to act/play together as I got older as she told me it was 'part of growing up and learning to stand up to the bullies and other people who deserve it' so I started punching her back and calling her names too which made my mum smile and laugh and appear very happy but strangely the people in street looked at us and you could see they thought we were properly fighting and looked at us with such disgust on their faces, sometimes the older people would say something under their breaths or worse to my mum, she'd just laugh and say nooo I love my daughter, we are messing she would then turn to me and say Emma tell the lady how funny you find it, I'd just nod and laugh knowing not to say different, i was very confused and asked my mum once we was on the bus why that lady thought we was hurting each other when we was just playing, don't all mummies do that? My mum then laughed and told me they was being nosey and ignore them as some people don't think it's the right way but they also think a lot doesn't mean they are right, I am your mum and you do as I say and no one else... Right!... I wish I could say that was end of it but the more people said something to her about it the more it seemed to encourage my mum to do it and before long it be-

31

came a daily 'bus stop game' and it was like she loved the attention she got from it. She was always so careful to never hit me hard enough to leave any marks though.

MY MUM'S NEW 'LODGER'!

Only a short while later maybe even only a few months after moving into the flats, my mum started hanging out with a new friend called Hazel who my mum apparently went to school with as a teenager and one of the friends she got back in contact with while helping out at my old school way before I ended up living with my nanna so god knows how she was back in touch with her now but this was the first time I had heard anything about this 'Hazel' though which I found strange, At first I thought she was a lovely person she involved me in everything they did she also talked to me and treat me fair, I'd describe Hazel as quite a large woman at a size xl waist at least and around 5ft 4" with brown wavy hair and glasses I thought oh lovely this is someone else who accepts me and my mum as a package... How wrong was I if only I could have predicted the future!

Once Hazel moved in with us into the 2 bedroom flat we lived in there was me in my own bedroom and Hazel and my mum in the other bedroom sharing a room with 2 single beds in, but the best thing was Hazel had a child too called Breeze!

Great a friend and someone to play with possibly I could be a big sister too as she was only a few years younger but a big girl so looked my age and was actually taller than me, how perfect my first ever friend since I had been forced to stop staying at my nanna's!

I remember Breeze well she was quite big for her age she was about 4 years younger than me maybe around 5 or 6 years old at this time, She had long dark brown hair and a round face with freckles but Breeze never lived with us full time, she lived with her nanna in the village we used to live, she visited and stayed over at the weekends though and it was like having a younger sister, life once again for a short while seemed liveable and good fun even, Yes I had to share my mum but this time it was worth it or so I thought! To say things went terribly wrong would be a huge understatement.

Hazel moved in with us because she was having serious 'adult' issues at her old home where she used to live with Breeze and her mother and step dad and her grandad all lived in a 4 bedroom house, her stepdad (Harry who was her mums husband the bloke who had raised Hazel as his own kid since she was a young age) and Hazel were having an affair or had been I wasn't sure at this time (well I worked out as much from overhearing conversations as kids do but aint supposed to hahaha) and Breeze was his daughter which made Hazels Step dad Breeze's Grandad and Dad too!

Well it seems rumours had spread in the village over many years of them having the affair and her own mother had just had enough of Hazel always trying to take over her mums house or something like that and she too had started to believe the rumours, I'm unsure of what trouble exactly was going off apart from that but the whole of Hazel's family was involved and it was bad, very bad and my mum informed me Hazel would be moving in for a little while until she found her own place to which I had no say in but I was fine with it, after all, she was there all the time n never did really leave so what difference was it to make to me if she was staying over a few weeks or for a long time? I never got any say in anything anyhow, I knew by now kids should be neither seen nor heard if at all possible this much my mum had shown me in her actions!

Life for the first few years of Hazel moving in was ok, I guess quite fun really, we had day trips out places on bus trips one favourite of my mum and Hazels was to get a bus day trip from a local tour operator that ran Mystery tours I later found out they got cheap day trips as Hazels brother was the bus driver so hardly cost them anything, we had holidays to Withernsea in Hazels mothers caravan she would let us use for the week at times.

All this was not to last though as I soon learnt Hazel had a temper at first it was just silly argument's between Hazel and her family and Hazel seemed upset a lot, I felt sorry for her and tried to offer her cuddles but she didn't seem to want me near her it was as though she'd made an effort wormed her way in got close to my mum and that was that job done!

Well, Hazel had lived with us in Sandbeck house a 2 bedroom flat for about 2 years now and I would've been around 10 maybe 11 roughly I am not good with dates and ages. On return home from a day out we was walking, laughing and discussing the day we'd just had, there was me, my mum and Hazel we wasn't far from home at all just on the subway system that led from the town onto our estate, on the way up the stairs from the subway, very close to our home my mum suddenly winced in pain and could not walk right at all, she struggled to get back to our flat and walked with a limp, I don't recall my mum going into the hospital or to the doctors or anything really she was just resting a lot and in a foul mood.

I do remember her a few months later my mum calling me into the living room one day after school telling me to sit down and then declaring she had been diagnosed with Multiple Sclerosis (MS) I didn't really fully understand what this was and only thing I was told is that it meant my mum would be sick more and may end up in a wheelchair and I had to grow up and help out around the house more, to stop being awkward like I was at times and keep my room clean and do more housework and shopping and whatever else was asked of me without moaning about it as she did not need it right now and after all the nice times we have had thanks to Hazel it was the least I could do now to help out and say thank you in actions.

I do not remember much about this time I was being bullied at school quite badly though I always tried to stand up for myself as my mum would be mad if I did not and I got into fights often and now with this, my head was a mess, I hated what I looked like and hated what clothes I was made to wear, I had no say like children do now about what glasses I had (which were big red plastic ones think Deirdre off coronation street or other crazy big cheek covering glasses) or no say at all in how I got to style my hair which I clearly remember it being short as my mum had clearly stated suited me better as it was just like hers and gave me a nice little chubby face but I so wanted my hair long like all my friends and do not get me started on my school uniform with my mum not working she never did do any work really apart from the volunteering at my school years ago which she stopped after she reappeared from who knows where?

My mum had held no work since then, she had never held a job for long I think she did not like been told what to do very much, my mum much preferred being in control more than being given directions and instructions if anyone ever tried telling my mum what to do she would get so very angry and well erupt it was crazy, anyway with her not working the school uniform consisted of a government clothing the grant non-working people received at that time back in maybe early 1990s!

Only description I can give the clothing back then that I got given to wear and that's gross, uncool, looked cheap and everyone who wore these clothes got bullied as everyone knew these was the poor kids and this tied with what my mum was going through so much with her health, what I was going through too with the day trips stopped and with Hazel getting more angrier and drinking a lot and nobody giving any attention to me, my mum either on sofa asleep or in bed ill, I may as well not being around, well I didn't know what messed my head up the most, all I know is I missed things how they once was, I wanted to be happy again, I'd started to forget about life when we lived at Stanford but now I was starting to recall those same feelings again and could see life returning back to those days, I really hoped I was wrong.

◆ ◆ ◆

My mum and Hazel talked about how life was too hard in the flat, how the fire alarm going off all the time at stupid o'clock in the morning due to the communal bin shoots being set alight setting the huge metal bins on fire at the bottom and fire engines evacuating us all the time being on 8th floor this seemed to happen often and with only having stairs as only emergency entrance as obviously lifts cannot be used in emergencies we soon realised the flat we lived really wasn't suitable for my mums needs and they needed to move, so not long after this is exactly what happened.

We then moved again to a rougher part of the estate into a ground floor 3 story flat called Cadeby House as the 8th floor flat really was not suitable for my mums needs now that she had issues walking and needed a stick to get around and a wheelchair for longer distances and had been diagnosed with Multiple sclerosis and now found out she also had late effects of polio from when she contracted it when she was born in 1961 but growing up and to this point she never knew she had it.......Really .....????

Life at this time was alright but was not as perfect as it once was but by now I knew how to look after myself, I had too and I started going out a lot even though I knew no one in the area. I had to go out as the arguments at home caused me to feel so upset, parents think children do not know or understand what's going off but you do don't you?

The arguments were quite a normal thing in my home, Hazel would do something differently from how my mum used to do it and because my mum couldn't do it she'd get frustrated make a remark to Hazel about it and all hell would break loose, I didn't hang around home much once they started arguing or disagreeing it was enough been yelled at each day at school without hearing it at home too as Hazel would reach for the bottle often Baileys and she would drink the lot then get very angry and it scared me at such a young age.

One day when I was around 11ish, me and Breeze popped to the local shop it was only 2 minutes' walk from where we lived, I was in unusually high spirits as my mum had bought me a new white Adidas t-shirt and given the fact I didn't get much new stuff never mind designer or sports stuff so I was super proud of it and had it on, I was chatting away happily to Breeze and I tripped up on a raised pathing slab on the pavement and sort of fell forwards, I cannot really describe how I fell as it all seemed to happen so very fast, yet so slow at same time, but it sort of happened like this ...If you visualise this I was facing the shop at a roughly 45 degree angle, my home behind me, I looked downwards to see what I had just stubbed my toe on so my face was looking down at the ground, top half started moving forwards still as if i was mid step forwards I realise I actually am, my legs are still moving in the direction I was heading which unfortunately is straight at the corner of a brick wall that belonged to the shop around 2 feet away if that but instead of walking I was stumbling forwards head and top half forwards looking downwards bent at hips, legs straight but totally couldn't stop stumbling forwards only about 2 steps away was the shop corner I was moving quite fast why can't I stop...the brick wall which I collided with seconds later head-on while still looking down at the ground, I heard a loud crack noise and a thud...The force of my head hitting the wall and speed I hit it at made me stumble backwards upon my head from front near forehead to crown hitting the wall and force bouncing me backwards, I somehow managed to stumble backwards into Breeze and she held me upright as I stood straight upright and for a split second I thought to myself well that was a great thing to do.....not... I didn't really at that time feel at all scared, There was no pain and I definitely did not realise the seriousness of what had just happened, I soon learnt just how bad it was as I touched my head to feel for lumps n bumps while laughing and saying that was lucky huh Breeze but as soon as I touched my head and said those words I felt wet on my fingers and before I could move my hand downwards so I could look what it was, I felt whatever it was streaming down my forehead and face and saw it was BLOOD it was gushing down my forehead down my hand and face and by now my t-shirt was turning RED, Breeze screamed out loud and shouted she was going for help and ran back to my home to get my mum, I still felt strangely calm and still had no pain at all but I did not want Breeze to just run off and leave me!

I looked around unsure what to do, I spotted this old man around 80 ish or so years old maybe, I shouted at this old man to help me please but the area I lived was not the type of place were anyone took notice of a child my age which was around 10 years old and he carried on walking away saying no sorry I said please its serious I am bleeding badly he looked and carried on, seriously who does such a thing?

I decided it was best if I took my top off and held it to my head which was now throbbing slightly but otherwise felt ok, I then walked home or started to I got half way when my mum came into view, It must have only been 1 minute since I had my accident but by now and by the time I had walked back to my home my T-shirt my lovely new white t-shirt was totally red and not 1 part of it was white at all and blood was dripping everywhere, I was more bothered about my new t-shirt and fact my mum had just said she would have to bin it as it would not come out than how bad my head was, I had wanted the T-shirt for so long and has I hardly ever got anything at all never mind something I actually wanted it meant so very much to me and I knew I'd not get another either, well the ambulance arrived within minutes and after hours of waiting in the hospital's A&E waiting room in Doncaster and being told by the triage nurse that it was only a small cut at the front of my head no more than maybe an inch and they'd clean me up soon, they discovered upon cleaning my wound and moving my hair properly that I had actually split my head open from the front near my forehead right along my scalp to the back near my crown down the centre of my skull!

It was that bad the doctor while cleaning it had his fingers in my head down to his first knuckles the Distal Interphalangeal part of the fingers on both hands inserted into the cut cleaning it that's how long and wide it was, I remember looking upwards with my eyes as I was laid on my back on the hospital trolley and seeing his fingertips disappearing into my scalp as he cleaned the wound, I don't recall being in any pain or feeling scared I just remember being curious and asking him lots of questions and it occasionally feeling extremely cold as he cleaned it with something icy cold a liquid I believe was saline but don't take my word for that hahaha, after he had cleaned the wound, he explained he would have to put a special type of dissolvable glue in my hair that would break down over time but I was not to wash my hair until all the glue has dissolved and my wound had fully healed, to do the procedure and get me home quickly rather than staple my head closed which would mean lots of stress for me, pain and need theatre he would use this procedure where he would tie ty hair together in knots on top of my head and pull them tight which would pull my scalp together then he would apply the glue to the knots and repeat until all my head that was split open was done like this as it was too bad for stitches by time it was done I looked like sonic the hedgehogs little ugly sister!!

Even though it was safer and easier to meet new people back in the early 1990s and I looked like a very famous blue hedgehog for a short while which majorly affected my confidence or what little I had left, I soon made friends on the estate, I think my 'cool' hairstyle may have had something to do with it, looking back though I now wish I had stayed lonely, I got in with a bad crowd and I started being what is known now as a hoodie but without the hoodie, I started smoking not just tobacco either a homeless man used to sell pre rolled roll ups to all us kids, we thought it was soo cool and we all while high would go shop-lifting and I was generally looking back really not a nice person to know, thankfully trouble within the gang stopped me being part of it all rather quickly! I wish I could say that was it but I found out my mum's Multiple sclerosis was terminal she told me the doctors had stated she would quite probably be dead by the time she was 41!! She was at this time in her early 30's not even old and I was overwhelmed by my emotions I was upset, confused and worry engulfed me. I kept this all bottled up and inside me as I had learnt to do.

Aged around 11 I stopped hanging around with the gang and decided I should be around my mum more helping her out if she was going to die I wanted as many memories I could with her and I wanted her to be safe and combatable, I started going shops for her as was local to town centre and keeping my bed-room tidy and cleaning the bathroom etc. It wasn't much but every little helps right?

Not long after this I had another accident that meant more time off school, I was quite a clumsy kid any how I had always been but this time I had a serious football Injury I obtained when I was trying out for the local under 16s girl team, The day I tried out it was icy and very muddy and I slipped during a tackle and twisted my knee which resulted in me tearing my ligament behind my knee, I ended up with it strapped up for weeks but it didn't get any better and I ended up needing surgery as it was dislocating on me while I was running or playing or doing sports and wasn't healing by this time I had it strapped for 6 weeks and once the bandage had come off had physio but it still did not help at all and I was in agony daily as the dislocation was happening more and more the Dr's sent me for further tests x-rays and such and then the specialist I saw informed me and my mum that my knee ligament had not healed and I needed a operation known as key hole surgery to try and fix my ligament which I soon had but the operation did not work and I carried on having knee dislocation issues and my specialist whom I was under at the time informed my mum with my knee dislocating there was a very high chance with how my knee was twisting to side I would need a knee replacement operation quite possibly before I was 21 years old, I felt my whole life was over, I was always falling over and I soon learnt through sheer frustration how to put my own knee cap back into place, this hurt a lot but not as much as it hurt when was dislocated so I preferred to put it back in place and lessen the pain myself rather than wait ages for help if help even came, I learnt quite a few times help did not always appear or I would be ignored when I asked for help, that is why I learnt how to do it myself luckily I somehow got it right yes it hurts but least it doesn't totally ruin my life it just swells up afterwards but soon eases upon resting it after a few days.

WOULD WE EVER SETTLE
IN ONE PLACE?

A few months later we again moved, this time into a nice new build bungalow from a housing association on a warden scheme estate to make things easier for my mum at yet another new area of Doncaster it was a small village called Skellow It was now 2 quite long bus rides to get myself to my school I had to catch a bus from Skellow a 10 minute walk from my home at 6am then travel to Doncaster a 40 or so minute bus ride, then walk across town centre which was always quite empty at 7am in the morning and eerie to get to the other bus station as back then there was the Southern Bus station and the Northern bus station for yes you guessed North and South areas of Doncaster that was in roughly late 1980's early 1990s I then had to catch the number 250 bus to Tinkle and get off after a roughly 45 minute trip at Hayfield to the school I attended and then walk another 10 minutes or so just to get there in time then at home time I would make the reverse trip back each day It was exhausting and I would often not get home until turned 6pm, but yet again it didn't make my mum or Hazel happier or their lives easier at all and certainly didn't make mine any easier with extra walking with my knee and how tired I was I felt extremely upset, in fact, it was the start of yet even worse things to come!

◆ ◆ ◆

Aged around 12 years old and living in a new Village, where again I knew no one and dragged away from the people I had got to know and the area I knew and felt safe in, I yet again became withdrawn and stressed and to make matters worse my grand-dad who for some reason my mum never took me to see often so I missed dearly had recently died after being murdered by an axe to the mouth, my close friend my best friend the only one I'd ever had and trusted so much was one of the people accused of doing the vile act though police wasn't pointing the finger it was just my mum whilst talking to Hazel and she wouldn't say such things if was not true, yes a 12-year-old girl murdering an old man and for what a few pounds IF the rumours was true at this point I choose not to believe them I mean Rachel was my best friend, she wouldn't!

I was in high school now in year 8 I was 12 years old and it was first period one morning in class when I completely lost it when Rachel turned to me in class and told me she had done this horrible crime, I still remember the horrific moment like it was yesterday!

I was sat at the back of the class on the right-hand side next to Maisy, Rachel and someone else was in front of us on the next table, Rachel just turned to me and said 'Emma I have something to tell you, I am the one who killed your granddad it was me but I never killed him I was there but it was Helen who had hit him with the axe' well to say I was gobsmacked was a understate-ment and I admit I saw red and started attacking her and anyone else who got in my way I was soo angry, I'd never felt this way ever before, I am not a violent person at all but I just lost it I can't explain it I just didn't realise at the time what was happen-ing at the time I was too hyped, angry and seemed to be acting on auto pilot way to out of control for me to realise how I was acting but afterwards as I sat in the heads office I realised just what I had done, I had attacked most children in my class who got between me and Rachel to protect her most of whom were my friends and I even hit 3 teachers that I liked and respected, I did feel utter shame in myself, I got excluded from school and my mum then put me into a new high school and I became part of the bully gang so to speak I never actually bullied anyone that is not my nature to be honest I just wanted friends, but news had spread about what I'd done at my last school and the school bullies latched onto me thought I were like them... GREAT...NOT!

I wasn't happy at this school being it was at other side town and syllabus was different they expected me to re-sit year 8 when I was in year 9! I started with anxiety and panic attacks as I did not wish to be part of this 'amazing' gang who everyone was scared of I wanted to do my studies make nice friends and have a quiet peaceful school day, life at home was loud and manic why would I want that at school too?

My mum had started driving and got herself a small gold metro and she would drive me to the school gates to drop me off and I would go in the main gates across the field towards the back of the school and across the pit top and I would hide in the community centre on our estate most the day or walk the streets etc., well this continued for a while until my mum caught me one day as I thought my mum and Hazel was going shopping so I went home for a drink and got caught, I ended up being home tutored and that was end of my education as she took me out of school stating I could not cope with it and telling me it was because I hated crowds and was fearful which somehow I suddenly started feeling was true and I started having panic attacks, this still puzzles me how she was able to do this to me? Make me believe I was scared of crowds as before that I was fine, it's amazing the power a parent has over a child's mind huh!

It was quite a while by the time I was assigned a home tutor and kept being given work I had done in the previous years to do when I finally did get one, I got bored and refused to do any of it, what was the point I knew I'd never pas a single exam at this rate and I told my tutor this, to which point she replied unless your mum has £250 per exam you will not be taking them and given I am only qualified in science it's doubtful you'd pass any anyhow, I felt utterly defeated and thought to myself what will I do as an adult now, how will I work, How will I go college, I suddenly felt I had no future.

NO SCHOOL, NO REAL FRIENDS, NO LIFE

I started hanging out on the streets and meeting people and quickly started talking to anyone I could I was that bored and lonely, some of which were much older than me, others my age but none stayed around after meeting my mum and Hazel for long some only called for me and never did ever again, my so-called home was no place to be in half the time as the arguments between my mum and Hazel were turning physical now not just verbal, Hazel was drinking a lot and my mum was constantly angry, I was often caught up in the middle.

I remember one very bad time, I don't recall much of it how it started, or why but my mum had suffered a stroke and was paralysed in bed from the neck down she'd told me that morning about her stroke, how it'd took her strength and how she wasn't able to move her legs and how it had made her arms and upper body very weak to point she really struggled to move them and how my mum would need to sleep a lot and she needed me and Breeze to be on our very best behaviour for a little while, I promised my mum I would do my very best, me and Breeze went back through to the front room and resumed watching TV.

A little while later I heard them arguing in the bedroom, I went in to tell Hazel not to start with my mum when she was so ill. It was then I first saw just how evil Hazel really was this will always haunt me in more ways than one, Hazel was leaning over my mum strangling her I freaked out shouted for Breeze to come and we both started trying to pull Hazel off my mum, Hazel is no small lady and since moving in had only got larger in size!

We were both yelling at her to stop and leave my mum alone! Hazel slapped Breeze to the floor and I ran away and Hazel turned and then came after me calling me a little B***H and saying she would sort me out first, then her precious daughter then my mum!

I ran to the intercom and pulled the alarm (we lived in sheltered housing a place for elderly and disabled and had a community warden and an intercom system that went straight to her office or home in emergency situations only was it to be used) Helen answered (our warden) and I started asking for help at which point Hazel told Helen I'd pulled it being naughty and was seeking attention and how sorry she was Hazel was now glaring at me with evil eyes yet sounded soo very calm in her voice and Helen said ok then cut off. Hazel then grabbed me by the throat and started squeezing I remember me telling her she was not squeezing hard enough as I could still breathe and talk and to squeeze tighter please, In fact I dared her to squeeze tighter, I had already started suffering from anorexia at that point and wanted to die anyway what was the point in living in a total hellish nightmare of violence and abuse with no escape and no respite from it not even school?

My mum suddenly appeared (Thinking back actually that is quite strange don't you think? Considering only minutes ago she was unable to move) and pulled Hazel off me and at that point Hazel looked horrified and ran out the room and she disappeared for a few hours, I spent that time in my room sobbing my heart out not understanding what had just happened or why it'd turned so hostile, my mum never did come in to my room and give me a cuddle or check I was ok etc. but I am sure she could hear me sobbing my heart out.

That was to be the start of many years of physical abuse in my life, my first meeting with the most horrible word beginning with A! I started going out a lot more after this event, I just didn't want to be at home it seemed like the violence and Hazel drinking was a daily occurrence recently, I had a mountain bike and would go out over the fields for bike rides during the day and I saw this lad looking at me on his motorbike well cross bike I got shy and started to ride off and I noticed there was about 4 of them now and as I didn't know them, I started to head home and noticed they were following me! I rode faster and faster reached my estate and they were on my tail I didn't want them knowing where I lived I also didn't want Hazel seeing me with them even though I was trying to escape she'd never see it that way I went through the estate square a tight part in middle of all the bungalows on the footpath It was so very hard to get through on a bike so they'd struggle more, It worked I took it fast and lost them in the maze of the estate got home and yes you guessed it Hazel had seen and hit the roof, another argument entails!

She's not even my mother so what gives her the right to lord it over me!! I don't know how or why but the argument suddenly went from me being called names such as stupid and immature, pathetic and nothing but an inconvenience and endangering myself to Hazel and my mum arguing about the dog not being walked?

I was so upset, hurt and thought if i can't have mates, got nothing apart from a bike, a TV to entertain me... what exactly was I supposed to do all day? I didn't go school, too young to work, had no mates as Hazel scared them all away and basically I was isolated and again felt very much alone, I'd wonder around the village on my bike, smiling at anyone who would show me bit of kindness, all I wanted was someone to talk to.

START OF SOMETHING BEAUTIFUL?

I think not! It was then aged 13 and a half I met Barry who was to become my boyfriend unfortunately, I was out on my bike and heading to shop for my mum and this guy who looked way older I'd guess 18ish wolf whistled across the road, I stopped my bike, looked around and he shouted in my direction I'm whistling at you babe, I smiled and went in the shop, Upon coming out he was there near my bike, he explained his mum knew my mum as his mum as his mum Susan cleaned at the community centre and we should be friends too and would I like to go Ice Skating with him now? I explained I had no money and doubt my mum would pay for me or allow me to go, He offered to pay and come ask my mum so I stupidly said yes, we went home and my mum shockingly agreed, in fact she smiled and seemed extremely happy about this!

I on bus on way to the Dome to go Ice Skating when I asked Barry how old he was, I was told by him that he was 19 but had learning issues which made his mind younger, ok fair enough he was older but that is the fun part is it not? A way to annoy your parents or that was my plan literally I wasn't interested in boys at all, I'd never even kissed a boy before this, I at this point was still playing with Barbie's and more interested in writing and drawing, having being home schooled I guess I was way behind mentally. You see I seriously thought if I went off the rails my mum would then have to pay me the attention I so desperately craved!

My mum actually really liked Barry and on first meeting asked me if he had an older brother! We dated for only a short period of time before I found out I was pregnant imagine it aged 13 and a half and pregnant it was 1997!

I didn't even want to have sex never mind understand what it was, I had never seen my mum with a guy for many years and when Billy was around they never touched each other not even a cuddle really the most I ever saw them touch was when Billy gave my mum a kiss on the cheek, I didn't know any boys nor had any boyfriends before meeting Barry, I did not understand what a relationship was or what sex was this was not the type of thing my mum told me about!

I thought it just what happened when you got a boyfriend and knew sex led to babies but that was it really, Barry told me it was natural and nothing to be scared of and everyone does it, I told him no and he got very upset and cried and I turned all confused not knowing how to respond at all and I simply left Barry room and I went home, my mum asked why I was looking upset, I told her what had just happened and that I didn't understand why he was crying and got so upset did I do something wrong and my mums response was oh love that's normal, It's expected of you, If you want to make him happy then you HAVE to do whatever he asks of you, that's how relationships work, it's all part of growing up and he's lovely, you do not want to lose him so I am telling you just listen to him ok, so tomorrow you go around and put it right, ok sweetheart now get ready for bed.

The next day I went around to Barry's he only lived 2 minutes from mine, I explained to Barry what my mum had said and he got a huge smile on his face and said see I told you all I want to do is make you happy. I remember the first time though I wish I didn't, I'm not going to go into details but it was not romantic or special at all, he actually put a video on said he'd show me what to do first an image/video of naked men and women appeared on screen, They was touching each other, kissing etc. and I recall feeling sick and thinking eeeewww that looks horrible and not at all nice, I don't want to do that!!!! Well i didn't but Barry did and my mum had made it clear I was to make him happy as was expected of me so I did exactly what he wanted, I knew what he was showing me was wrong but also felt curious at first until he started touching me I stood up to leave and walked out the door he then started crying and saying if I didn't try it how would I know if I liked it, He also said my mum liked him very much and that I didn't want to make her mad, which was true I didn't and lesser things had made her mad as his mum had told him, so I agreed to do as he wanted and I rushed home soon afterwards and had a very hot bath, I felt dirty and confused and hurt as if this was normal why did I feel like this, I sat in the bath and thought maybe everyone feels like this, maybe it's just how it is? I felt calmer at this thought and got out the bath a little happier.

My mum must have known what we were up to that day as Barry's mum Susan worked at the community centre as a cleaner and her and my mum were friends and Susan was at my mums saying noises from that room and has Susan obviously knew what we had done that day and said that my mum said so you actually for once listened then, I replied Yes and went to my room and cried quietly cuddling into my teddy for comfort. Susan was just as bad as my mum really she didn't care either about what went off in her house, her younger son was the same age as me, he was called Phil, he took drugs, as I found out one day when he offered me some white stuff, I refused, she must've told my mum as the next day my mum questioned me and said "Emma you have a smile on your face (no i didn't I had not smiled since I had sex) I know what you're up to" and then she laughed and said good on ya girl, I am proud of you but remember to make him happy and do anything he asks! So here I was not yet 14 and pregnant with abusive household at home no one to turn to and in a relationship I did not even want to be in or fully understand but was scared to leave you see Barry too was quite a big guy and sometimes shouted at me then afterwards told me he was sorry but I made him do it so that must be right like my mum has always said I made her and Hazel shout at me and they'd not do it if I behaved, and my mum had told me to treat Barry right and make him happy so all this him shouting must be my fault? I was in my first ever relationship I'd not even had any kisses or owt before this! I finally told my mum I was pregnant and she shockingly congratulated me but only after saying she hoped Barry was going to stand by me............

That was it me stuck in a relationship I did not want to be in being told I had to get engaged to Barry now I was aged 14 and married once I turned 16 or else they would be trouble and I would fetch great shame upon the family and how the family would never ever accept it if we did not marry, this is what she told Barry and me, he obviously agreed to do this i recall him saying yes mother, I'm going nowhere mother, I'll always look after her. I felt trapped scared and unloved from all directions!

Death seemed an option but my baby inside me is the only thing I lived for, I knew it wasn't this baby fault and I knew nothing about abortion I honestly thought keeping it was only option to me! I did not see my nanna much around this time, but oh how I wish I did, I wish I could have had some way of seeing her and telling her how I felt but I lived 2 bus rides from her, had no money ever as my mum stopped my pocket money saying she needed to buy baby items and wedding stuff and an engagement ring!

A few weeks later we told Barry's family who did not like me or so I thought back then now I know they were trying to pro-tect me without bad naming their son more on this soon, his mum Susan went nuts and said do you know how old Barry is? I said of cause I do he is 19, at this point she started to laugh, she knew my age and told me he was 23 obviously I laughed thinking she was a mad cow and trying to split us up so I would get into trouble with my mum why else would she suddenly be saying this?, Susan then got his birth certificate to show me and I saw date of birth and worked out he was in fact 23 years old! Yes, you read right 23 and Susan had allowed him to take me up to his bedroom in his mum's house where he lived and have unlawful sex and now she was yelling at me? I should point out at this point Barry had a learning issue, he acted like he was my age mentally! So here I was pregnant and stressed to max and now being told this young lad was in fact a MAN!

I was smiling on outside telling everyone what I thought they wanted to hear as I was too fearful to do otherwise. I was scared of what my mum, Hazel and Barry and rest of my family would say/ do and think of me, but I was hurting so badly on the inside, life was so very bad, I didn't want any of this, I just wanted to be happy, Instead I was being sick every morning, felt sick all day, couldn't eat the foods I enjoyed and life was just bad.

The arguments between my mum and Hazel seemed to calm at least, there was a new focus now and everything seemed ok until I was a few months pregnant and there was yet again a massive argument I can't remember details but I do remember me walking in front door with Barry and Hazel shouting at my mum, I said oh gosh not again can we please stop, I have a baby coming in a few months, I don't want this around my child, this enraged Hazel who then turned flew at me and slapped me and force of her backhanded slap knocked me on my bum to the floor!

Luckily the baby and I were fine, even though I was never taken to be checked out at hospital nor DRs I felt the baby move and had no pains in my stomach area luckily she'd lashed out at my face, I mean how could she take me to get checked she would have a dam hard time covering that one up!

I remember the first appointment with the midwife, her asking me if I had agreed to sex obviously I said yes but she'd asked me in front of Barry and my mum, what else could I say? They were both glaring at me and I was scared to explain how it had really happened, that was that nothing more was asked, the midwife smiled looked at my mum said and you're ok with this? My mum said Yes obviously I am going to support them and it's all ok and smiled, the midwife then carried on with the appointment I thought what...so this is lawful it is normal?

I was praying desperately it wasn't and hoped so much that they'd be a knock at the door soon enough for the government or police or someone to protect me, well for anyone to really but that knock never came so I took it that all this was in fact 100% legal and that my mum, Hazel and Barry was indeed right, This is normal after all that everyone who told me it was bad was wrong and that my mum was right like my mum was telling me everyone who was being nasty about us or saying it was wrong was just jealous I'd found someone at my really young age when others do not find love that young if at all sometimes and that rest my life was sorted out now and I would not have to ever worry and how I should be thankful for that and stop looking so dam grumpy!

THE REALITY OF BEING
A TEEN MUM!

A ged 15 in April 1998 just 5 months before my 16th birthday I gave birth to a little boy whom I named Dean he was 7lb 11oz and I adored him, he really was the apple of my eye but being so young and with me being depressed already I sadly suffered from postnatal depression but this was not diagnosed until I was having my babies 6-month check-up by which point my mum was already helping look after Dean and doing most of his basic care, she noticed I was struggling and started taking over, making my babies bottles, washing his clothing, bathing him etc. etc. I honestly felt pushed out like the baby was hers and Hazels not mine at all, she joked and said to people I was the surrogate mother, I wasn't sure what this meant and when I asked my mum she laughed said oh it just a joke… cheer up ffs!

Throughout the day I would care for my son to the best of my abilities which in all fairness was not that good given fact I could not do much as my mum and Hazel was doing everything before I had chance and fact I had no clue how I mean I had never been taught how to look after myself, how to wash or style my hair properly, how to dress right or even what suited me but I did try my best to do what I could for my son and at night my mum would take over, she's not all bad my mum can be the most loving caring and the sweetest person going sometimes!

Life continued in a haze of bottles, nappies, puke and me sleeping a lot, I honestly do not recall much of this time, I wish I did,

I really do, my abuse continued though, I wasn't happy at all but acted as though I was so I did not too upset anyone else, I just did what was expected I learnt if I put out when he wanted me to and had sex with him it hurt less, but i never once wanted to do so, for one I didn't want to get pregnant again and he would not use condoms as he said they made him itch!

I got my own place at 15 years old and moved in with Barry, well it wasn't my place, my mum and Barry went to the council and explained the situation and they got us a 3 bedroom house in Doncaster in a place called Hyde-Park the house was on a street called Childers Street it had 2 rooms downstairs and a cellar, I hated that dark, cold cellar so much it would become a place I feared and the start of me hating enclosed spaces, the council knew my age 15 years old and Barry's which was 25 at time and gave us a house to live as a couple but the benefit office informed Barry he would need to claim the only benefit you could claim child benefit which was only benefit for children back then which he had to claim for both me and our baby, Yes you read that right Barry was expected to claim for me as my guardian and was now legally responsible for me until i was 18 years old so he was both my boyfriend and my well I guess legal guardian/adoptive father in eyes of the law anyhow!

My mum told us we needed this house now as I was told it was for best and that I needed to move out as you see I was pregnant again unplanned and again result of rape and coming up to 16 years old, so we moved into this house but my mum refused to let me take my son, telling me if I took him from her now after almost a year it would most certainly kill her as she'd be so upset and the upset with her MS would or could easily cause a heart attack or stroke which with sever upset possibly would kill her and if that is what I wanted then fine, go ahead and take Dean, obviously it was not what I wanted, I wanted my son but

I did not want my mum dead! Even though I didn't wish to I left Dean with my mum, I saw Dean as much as I possibly could do so but being a bus ride away and me being pregnant and trying to get furniture and house ready for this baby arriving I could not get through as much as I would have liked, my gosh I missed Dean so very much it really did feel like part of me was missing constantly.

The wedding planning continued, my mum took control I honestly showed no interest at all when choosing flowers, food, dress and rest of preparations needed for the wedding when asked I just said whatever and smiled sweetly, we got married on June the 3rd 1999 at Doncaster Registry Office, even though I did not live with my mum at the time I still felt I had to marry Barry after all its what everyone was saying was the right thing to do and how would fetch great shame upon the family if i didn't and how my son would be a bastard and that'd not be right in school now would it!

I was made to feel, trapped scared and isolated and I still feared my mum and now Barry too and did as they both told me to do and pretended to be happy. My mum took me shopping bought me a wedding dress well it was a summer dress white lace with a white matching lace jacket the dress went just above my knee that she had chosen as I had no interest in the wedding at all I would have happily worn my jeans and a t-shirt, It must've been obvious I didn't wish to as i didn't exactly show any interest in any of the preparations or detailing at all, she in fact organized everything every little detail it was not my wedding it was hers in all but name and all that my wedding day should entail such as flowers, entertainment, venue was chosen by my mum and Hazel.

Along with the dress my mum had chosen I had a red teardrop artificial rose arrangement for the bouquet and the venue for after party was the community centre were we lived, the wedding would be at the register office and my mums friend May a resident on the estate her son did the photo's as a wedding present, we had no cars just my mums with a ribbon on it which by now she had a white Peugeot 106, So on 3rd July 1999 I got married in a register office in Doncaster, I cried as soon as I walked into the Register office, everyone in my family kept telling me it was just nerves or cold feet and to stop being daft and wipe my eyes and wear a smile. I sobbed all the way through as I said my vows not out of happiness but out of fear and self-hatred that I had no strength to run away or speak up and say No i bloody do not, I was scared of what would happen if I did, so instead I took the vows and felt utterly defeated.

TEENAGED MARRIED LIFE!

I went on to have a second baby boy whom I named Rory who was born prematurely at 28 weeks pregnant in September 1999 thankfully my mum was still looking after Dean, I tried to move him in with me a few months before but it was my mum he saw as his mum not me she was the one he wanted when upset I could not settle him which even to this day it stings and hurts like mad that and with what my mum had said regarding how it'd kill her if I took him away from her now and I didn't wish any harm upon my mum I mean she was now 35 and doctors had already said she'd be dead by 41, so yet again what could I do but leave him with my mum, can you imagine the pain that causes if not I'll tell you, I felt like I was incomplete, I felt my baby should be with me, my arms and heart ached to hold my boy, I felt heartbroken all these feelings alone just because my son wasn't with me, then I felt guilt immense guilt at how selfish I was being at even considering fetching my son home and trying him again when I knew It would possibly kill my mum, could I really live with that guilt of knowing if she died it was because of my actions, yes I would have got my son home but It'd killed my mum, so I thought about it over and over and each time I cried and just couldn't do it, I knew if I took my son my mum would die and I'd be to blame and I was pregnant again I had to think about this and do the right thing for my children not what was right by me and I decided I would let my mum raise Dean even though I was terribly upset at reaching this decision and I honestly trusted I was doing right thing, I told my mum and she was sooo very happy and Barry seemed happy at decision being reached too. I had again managed to made everyone around me happy but not myself, usual story their then, no wonder I had Rory so prematurely I was so very stressed and constantly trying to prepare for the birth of my baby, look after the house, do shopping, deal with my mum and Hazels dramas, be there for Dean much as I could be and everything else in-between that needed doing.

My baby Rory bless him was born so very tiny and he had quite a few major health issues he was on a life support machine and in an incubator, he was only 2lb 1oz and his skin was transparent and was as small as my hand, even the premature baby nappies I were given by the Special Care baby unit at DRI in Doncaster were way too big for him they covered his bum right up to his ribs bless him, It was extremely hard seeing my poor baby in so much a fragile state, that very first night of his life I was told I might wish to get a vicar in and call the family to say goodbye, I simply said no chance my baby not going anywhere he's a fighter!

I sat up all night by the incubator, holding my babies tiny little hand, well putting my finger into his palm and using my thumb to gently stroke his arm whilst talking to him and willing him to pull through, but at 3am the machines around him started bleeping, the nurses and Dr's ran into the room and quickly ushered me out the room, I was in tears, confused and scared, the nurse reappeared after only a few moments but it seemed like ages and she asked me to go back inside the room and explained to me that Rory is ok but that he had suffered a stroke and a mini heart attack and they needed to give him a blood transfusion, his poor skin was so bruised from where they'd done cpr and his arms bruised from where they had inserted the drips and taken blood, it really was so horrifying!

Once again I was told he may not make the night and really

should prepare for the worst, I sat by his incubator again and did not move from his side, Was I scared oh boy yes very much so, I had very little support around me, the only support i had that night was the nurses really I don't recall Barry being there, I don't even know if he was or not my attention that night was solely on Rory, but Rory pulled through and survived his first night I just knew he would!

◆ ◆ ◆

I remember the main support I got was from the medical staff there who truly were amazing and definitely do not get enough praise for what they do daily, with their help I soon learnt how to bathe him because he couldn't leave his incubator yet I had to use cotton wool balls and warm water and wash him inside the incubator which was fiddly and was worrying as there was so many tubes and wires and not much room at all, they also taught me how to feed him through his feeding tube that went up his nose and was taped to his cheek as he kept pulling it out so they also showed me how to sort this should it happen again and they taught me how to change his tiny little nappy inside his incubator, oh my god how tiny the nappies were and even the smallest size buried him! At only 2lb 1oz you can imagine my horror every time I had to touch him, I wanted too so badly but was so scared I'd hurt him as his skin which was almost transparent so much so you could see the blood pumping through his veins, his arms and legs so very thin I felt if I touched them too hard they'd break or bruise more it was terrifying but Rory started gaining strength and started gaining weight very slowly, Rory had so many health issues so early in his life he had a stroke, had a heart attack that first night and also a heart murmur and he had to have a blood transfusion and for first 2 months could not breathe unsupported but all the progress he was making was impressing the DRs and I am so very pleased to say though Rory made a full recovery and while Rory was in hospital I got another house for us to live as the house I had at moment was ok but it was so far from my mum I just could not settle plus that cellar, I did not like it at all I was often instructed to go down there and always refused so Barry would get angry, yell at me and put me through the door at top of stairs that led to cellar then he would closer the door and hold it closed, One time I was down there for over a few hours, I was at time pregnant with Rory and in a state, I was crying, needing toilet and hungry too and so thirsty I was banging on door, shouting at the little grate hoping someone outside would hear me but we lived at bottom of street no one hardly passed our house, it was no good, I was trapped in this dark cold freezing cellar and didn't know how long for, Eventually Barry let me out and told me I would face that every time I did not listen to him and he meant it too!

The council agreed to move us closer to my mums and so while Rory was in hospital I started packing, visiting Rory, coming home more packing with Barry being no help at all as per usual and more often than not arguing or insisting on me making him happy as if I had time or energy for that right now but he was not taking No as a reply he never did! So for next few weeks this was my life and finally we got the keys and could move and get the house which was a 2 bedroom Terrence house in Highfields in Northern Doncaster only 1 short bus ride to my mums and meant I could see Dean more too and now we could get the house ready for Rory coming home and surprisingly out of blue only 1 week after getting the house keys we was told after Rory had spent a total of almost 3 months in hospital that he was allowed to come home, I was ecstatic as they'd said he would be in hospital until the New Year quite possibly but this meant Rory would be home for his first Christmas then reality hit you see the downside was where I'd moved to was damp, it had no boiler and was getting repairs done and was undecorated, had no carpets or radiators which because I thought Rory would be in hospital until new year I thought would not be an issue but now......

It was no place for a new born never mind a premature baby with under developed lungs and a heart murmur, I explained this to the hospital and they suggested maybe a relative could help us until house was ready and my mum yet again stepped right up and offered to watch him for me and have him at hers just until my house was sorted with no other option I agreed, I obviously visited him daily and spent many hours with him, Rory was about 7 months old by time house was sorted they were the worst months of my life, my heart ached when I was away from him and I couldn't sleep at all even though I was shattered, I kept wondering if he was ok, was he fed ok, did my mum know what to do and when I did fall asleep I woke up thinking I was hearing him crying I can't explain how it felt, my mum never once let me stay overnight with my baby even though I explained how hard it was for me she insisted I needed to go home to finish the house and I knew she was right.

I worked from 5am to 10 am doing the house up, decorating it, getting it ready then I would leave Barry to sort the workmen out and watch over them while I would catch the bus and go to my mum's then spend much time as I could with my two son's before returning home at 6pm as area I lived wasn't really safe after that to be out alone or I never felt safe living their overly and I would continue getting house sorted until 1 am, It wasn't for 4 months after this that I finally got my new heating working and carpets down, the house fully dried out and decorated, Carpets down and the ok to fetch my son home from the community health team that Rory needed for his care.

Rory came home at last and I loved being a full-time hands-on mum but I had no friends, No life outside being a mum and to be honest only Rory and Dean kept me going gave me a reason to live I had arguments every day If Barry didn't like what I was wearing or how I had my hair or didn't have tea ready on time it didn't matter that Rory needed a feed if Barry was hungry I was expected to sort his tea first and my babies too life was soo hard and demanding, even if I bought a toy for Rory or for Dean and I did not buy Barry anything at same time he'd get so jealous and start on me.

SO VERY TIRED

B een a full time teen mum is not as you expect at all it's hard work and challenging and given the fact that I was a teen mum to 2 children was by this point only 17 almost 18 and pregnant again, I should say not by choice either if I didn't 'put out' then that meant an argument or me being hit or worse him telling my mum I was not looking after him right which resulted in both my mum and Hazel starting on me, Barry did not like to use condoms and I was not allowed to use protection to be honest I didn't even at that time know what other protection there was, I was still very naive and immature in many ways and half the time he forced himself upon me although I never told anyone I was too scared too and any way Barry told me it wasn't rape as we were in married and it was his legal right as my husband to have sex with me.

In roughly end of 1999 my mum started talking about moving to Grimsby as she had always wanted to live nearer the seaside and so we too started planning a move to Grimsby as there was no way my mum was moving there taking Dean with her and leaving me in Doncaster miles away from my son Dean, there was no chance that was happening so Barry agreed we too would yet again move this would be our 4th place in only a few years together, I started feeling down again worse than ever I had a young baby a move to plan it was so stressful and so in early 2000 we moved to Grimsby, I lived at 94b and my mum at 96b Ainslie Street, Grimsby both of us in a ground floor flat we were neighbours and I must admit life seemed to be on the up, I was managing life more easily, I was feeling a whole lot more confident and happy in myself, I still was not getting along with Barry great obviously but I spent most my time at the local park just walking Rory in his pushchair for miles but this was short lived as always, the new neighbours we had really were complete nightmares the one upstairs in flat above us was a SAS soldier honest to god he was a total nut case who thought his word and his alone was right and used to love telling stories in front of my son I will add about his time in army and how many men he had killed with his bare hands and how he only wished he was still doing that today, one day I tried telling him he had a leak in his flat and it was coming through our bathroom light fitting he went nut's shouting screaming and telling me I was lying saying that he thinks he would know if he had a leak in his flat and not to be stupid! Barry I learnt on this day had a very short temper with others and not just me as all of a sudden Barry and the Ex SAS guy ended up in a fight, neither of them caring about the fact I had a baby in the same room who was seeing everything and I was again pregnant by this point too, typical! It was only when I threatened to ring the police did they both stop and the guy disappeared into his flat and I got it in the neck that night big style by Barry telling me 'who the hell do I think I am threatening to ring police on him after everything he has done for me I should be grateful for him saving my life' I seriously did not know if to laugh, cry or hit him, at this point in my life I was starting to think of a way out of the nightmare, I was 17 years old was still trying to come to terms with just finding out I was again pregnant only a few weeks earlier meaning I was going to have 3 kids by the age of 18!

This pregnancy was already causing me issues though I was bleeding on and off which ended up continuing throughout the pregnancy and I was often being rushed to the hospital via an ambulance each time totally scared stiff but on this occasion of me going toilet and seeing the blood I realised this was bad I seriously really concerned I was going to lose my baby, I'd never seen so much blood it was frightening and filling big thick pads quickly and again I was rushed into hospital and everything was ok so was again next day sent home after some bed rest and monitoring both me and baby, this happened a good few more times and I started to realise that it quite may be the stress causing this to happen and I realised for my children's safety and my sanity I had to save up and get out of the relationship but I was scared too scared to do it plus Barry always made sure I never had much money available there was always something he wanted often stupid thing's for himself such as a game or a game system but he'd throw a temper tantrum in the shop if I didn't get it or allow him to so it was not like I had any option any how I wish I had. I might have been one with money but he made it clear I was to spend it how he said or needed looking back I wish I'd had more strength!

In November 2000 I was yet again admitted to hospital with heavy bleeding this time they decided to keep me in for observation and complete bed rest until my daughter was born as they told me I had Placenta Previa and the Dr went on to explain that this is a condition where the placenta lies low in the uterus and partially or completely covers the cervix and the placenta may separate from the uterine wall as the cervix begins to dilate (open) during labour and this is what had possibly by looks of it happened to me so they wanted to keep a closer eye on me and bed rest until 36 weeks, I begged them to deliver her now as I had another very young and disabled child that needed me and I couldn't be bed bound for so long, plus I would go mental too with being so still and bored, surely that'd not be good for the baby inside me, I was 32 weeks pregnant and was very stressed and was scared this would hurt my baby but at first they refused to deliver her now as the baby was fine and showing no signs of distress, but the very next morning the same doctor came to see me and put the heartbeat monitor on my stomach and said he would be back soon, 30 minutes later he returned looked at the machine and walked away he came back only moments later and explained how the theatre had been informed and that I was being prepped soon and that I should ring who I want to go in with me as I was to go down soon, I was to have a caesarean section as my daughters heartbeat was irregular indicating the baby may be stressed, this obviously worried me and I don't really recall much after that it was such a blur of my mum arriving with Barry, then the Dr reappearing and saying something about how the special care baby unit was full, they had no incubators available due to an emergency they had just had rushed in and that I had a choice between Doncaster DRI or Manchester! I obviously choose Doncaster DRI as I for one had family there and second reason I knew the hospital and the area and I knew it was closest of the two so also the safest for me and mostly my baby, The next hour was a blur of me being in an ambulance, lights on sirens on and then arriving at Doncaster DRI and me getting wheeled straight down to theatre, being asked to lay on my side and catching sight of this very long needle for epidural going into my spine... owchie.... Then the sterile theatre, a sheet being put up and introduced to all these people in scrubs I didn't catch who was who as I was too scared to be honest.

I then saw Barry and laughed at state of him in the scrubs here's all the Dr's and midwifes all of them were looking quite smart and well sterile and clean then in comes this short fat guy holding his hands up in front of him a dopey look on his face his hair sticking out from under his hat in all directions in these long curly messy greasy locks he was walking across room saying 'ooooo aaayyyy we doing this, eeeeeyyyy' in this stupid squeaky voice he clearly found hilariously funny and pulling these ridiculous faces I wouldn't know how to describe if I tried too, I was told they was going to now start, I was scared but I was so relieved too I just wanted my daughter safe, I felt a strange sensation on my stomach like a scratching then a voice told me I will feel a little bit of tugging soon but then another voice spoke up saying my baby had turned and gone further up in my stomach and they was so sorry but they was going to have to cut vertically inside up to my naval on inside of my womb or something like this I was terrified but then I felt a strange tugging and unusual feeling in my stomach and only seconds later my baby daughter was born I asked the time and was told it was 10:10 am It was the 3rd November 2000 and my daughter weighed 3lb 2oz, I knew within the first few seconds of her life she was going to be a little handful as when the doctors lifted her from my stomach she grabbed the sheet/divider that was hiding my wide open stomach and pulled it down, I looked down thinking what the.... and couldn't help but laugh she had this look on her face I'll try to explain it imagine her eyes wide and lips in a pout that look on her face was like.......oooooooohhhh were, am I? The surgeons stitched me up with dissolvable stitches on inside and the ones on outside would need removing in 5 days' time!

I did not get to see my daughter for the next 3 hours, all I had was a photo of her which the fantastic team at Doncaster DRI fetched to me straight away as she needed help to breathe and was rushed to an incubator and rushed to the special care baby unit as she only weighed 3lb 2oz with jet black hair she was the most beautiful stunningly beautiful baby, even though she were tiny she had such chubby cheeks, unlike Rory my daughter skin looked normal colour and texture, apart from being small in length she looked otherwise healthy but her lungs was slightly undeveloped and she had a slight heart murmur but I was reassured this was nothing at all to worry about and because of Rory and how his birth was I knew my daughter would be fine.

I just wished I could be with her but I had stitches and until I was walking around they was not letting me leave the ward, by the end of that day I had the midwifes agreeing to take me to my daughter in a wheelchair as I was forcing myself to walk too much far quicker than the Midwifes liked as I wanted/needed to get to my daughter so much, Barry was useless and my mum was watching Rory while Barry was staying at my Nannas while we was in hospital in Stanford, so I didn't want my daughter all alone and Barry kept coming down and sitting with me saying he was bored up there, and there was nothing for him to do so why is he up there in the way? In the way.... He was sitting with his daughter, caring for her, what went through his mind sometimes? I often do wish I understood!

We was in Doncaster DRI for 3 days before I was told I could leave and the ambulance would be transporting Katie as I had decided to call my daughter to Grimsby special care baby unit that afternoon, I still had my stitches in and was scared of them bursting open, I asked if I could travel with my daughter and they told me a Dr had to travel and the 2 paramedics and driver so no sorry wasn't room, I had to find my own way there, I rang my mum and luckily she came straight through and collected me and I recall every bump in road was agony I was holding a cushion across my stomach and could not wear the seat belt, It was a 50 minute journey on the motorway at 70 mph to Grimsby from Doncaster and was sooo painful of a trip too, we arrived at Grimsby hospital and I was ushered into a sideward where they admitted me and gave me a swab for MRSA! I do panic too easily and started thinking worse hahaha! Turns out was just precautionary in the end and a few hours later I finally was reunited with my daughter.

Those next few weeks that followed were a blur of hospital visit's and trying to organize a Christmas for my other children, life was chaotic and manic and that along with my then so-called husband arguing and acting like a child himself made me very stressed, Good news did follow though the hospital had a room for me as Katie was due to come home yay! I had also got us a better newer home as the flat we lived in had so many issues it ended up condemned and luckily for me a local housing association gave us a 3 bedroom end Terrence house with a huge 21ft garden and 2 living rooms downstairs it was to me perfect family home and I set about decorating it along with everything else and it in end looked truly amazing, I was so happy to start with and this would become my home for the next 10 years.

The very next day after house was finished and I went to the hospital and I was told they had a family room I could have for 3 days as Katie was ready to come home and they thought it'd be a good transition and so I went home got all the items I needed and returned to the room and that night for the first time I got to care for my daughter all by myself, It felt like Heaven those first few hours with just my daughter and I no nurses breathing down your neck or just being around and no machines bleeping or alarms going off it really did feel like pure bliss and It was so perfect....or so I thought but a few hours later on that first night it must have been around 3am I went toilet and heard Katie cry so I flushed toilet walked out and she had gone silent so I checked on her and noticed her chest was still.... Katie had stopped breathing I hit the alarm on the wall and within seconds the nurses ran in and flicked the bottom of Katie's foot she started crying instantly it turns out she had an irregular heartbeat and a hole in the heart and would stop breathing in her sleep and it happens a lot to premature babies all I had to do was tickle her foot or flick the bottom of it gently to get her to respond and take a breath it really was totally terrifying and to reassure me the hospital gave us a special cot monitor for her to sleep on and if she stopped breathing the alarm would sound which obviously would awaken us and really helped me big style upon going home in those first few weeks.

I am happy to say Katie didn't have any more of these breathing doo's and the hospital took the mat off us which was terrifying as I would stay awake for long as I could scared that without this alarm she'd die while I was sleeping and I would not know and she would die luckily this did not happen and Katie made brilliant progress and Rory loved her and adored her too they were often mistaken for twins as they looked so similar in age by time Katie was 1 as Rory was growing very slowly due to his small birth weight he was only slightly bigger than her and they both looked the same age in the face etc. it was too cute, life seemed so perfect the arguments were still there but I had my children they were safe, happy and loved that is what matters right?

My happiness could come later I seriously thought that by plastering on a smile and making my kids happy, well-fed and looked after and by treating them, days out holidays etc. that they'd never know how sad mummy felt inside and I thought it was working, I mean my mum didn't know how I felt she thought I had accepted my life and was happy, Barry didn't know, Nobody did, I had learnt to hide my pain well and learnt my happiness was certainly not important.

When Rory was aged 2 ½ in 2001 I was offered a place for him in a child development group (CDC) a play group for children with special needs and I had more free time which was a great help not just to me but to Rory too, he seemed to really start and shine and his development was improving slowly, though by now he was falling behind his sister in his milestones, home life didn't improve at all and to be honest I did not want to be at home during this time so while Rory was in the CDC, me and my daughter would visit a friend I had made called Maria, It was then one day at Maria's house I met this man named Liam who lived near Maria, He wasn't anything to look at, He was around 5ft 6" of large build and had a round face with a ginger goatee and ginger shaved crew cut hair but he had a decent personality and we got along very well and soon I was going around to his and we ended up having an affair, I did not hide the fact from anyone I was really hoping Barry would find out and leave me a few months later he did find out and obviously he went crazy, Barry knew I was going there but he believed we were just friends even though I told him what was going off, he choose not to believe me thinking I was joking?

◆ ◆ ◆

One night after a pretty bad argument and him hitting me that day Barry randomly offered to look after the kids while I went out, which was I admit out of character for him but I agreed and so I put kids to bed then I went to Liam house but within 30 minutes of me arriving there was a loud banging at the back door, Liam was in the shower, I was watching TV in the living room I shouted through and asked Liam if he wanted me to answer the door he said to ignore it as it'd be kids they'd been playing knock a door run for a while now so I ignored it and the very next thing you knew Barry was shouting, I yelled oh shit and said two minutes this enraged Barry more and he started shouting louder now and sounding much angrier than I had ever heard him and was banging on the door I was scared he was going to kick it in so moved back, Liam flew out the bathroom opened the door with only his towel around him and invited him in, Barry started yelling and making threats, I was more concerned by the fact it was middle of winter and he'd fetched both my young toddlers out in a double push chair with no rain cover on and no bloody coats on so I hold him as much as I barged past them both and grabbed the push chair, I put the kids and buggy into my car and drove home leaving them both to it, I wasn't interested in anything but getting my poor babies back home and to bed, Barry arrived only 30 minutes later still angry and fuming but then as soon as I told him to shut up or leave he went silent never until this day had I ever had any courage to raise my voice back, He went on to ask me why I wanted another man and what was wrong with him, I told him because he treats me like shit always had done and I was only with him cause my mother made me do so and I never once wanted to be with him in any way and I actually do not like him at all and I wanted him out my life and his response was please don't leave me please, you can see anyone and do anything you wish but don't leave me, sleep with different men, do anything but please do not leave me.

My mum found out as Barry rang her and she came straight around and she also went nut's with me told me to think about the kids they needed their dad and I needed him, I honestly felt so lost, I told my mum what I had just told Barry and she said tough! You spread your legs, you can't do this, you're a mum, your kids need you, Barry needs you so grow fuck up and be a wife and mum before social services get involved and you lose your kids! This scared me so much, I'd heard of social services removing kids, knew it happened and was not going to let it happen, No I would do as I had all these years, I'd stay, I'd put my kids first and be a good wife, I went around to Liam house not long after and told him the news I'd since discovered.... I was pregnant!

Now I knew there was 99% chance It was not Barry's baby, I don't recall him raping me nor me sleeping with him in any way, shape or form around this time he was more bothered with his new passion 24 hours a day, he'd discovered internet chat groups and was talking to people on that, I presumed women and secretly hoped too that he'd find someone else and leave so I encouraged him to go online, enjoy I even bought him a webcam and mic so he'd spend more time in front room that he'd made his computer room where kids nor I was allowed in, he was in there from 7am to I don't know what time each day while I got on with my life, I lived as though I was single, Not once did I feel like I was in a relationship until I met Liam, Me and Barry may have shared a bed but I slept dressed! Arriving at Liam's I told him I was pregnant and highly likely the baby was his and asked him what he wanted to do about it and he told me he wanted nothing to do with the baby and that he was not wanting to per- use a relationship with me as it wasn't right nor fair on Barry! I hit the roof, said Barry, BARRY! what about the baby inside of me, I aint asking you to marry me, I aint asking you to be with me, I am though asking you to be a father to your child and be there for the baby as it's his life inside of me more than likely! Liam refused, said he was very sorry, I left went home, Told Barry what Liam had said, To which Barry replied, That is ok he will be mine, no one needs to know and I will raise him as my own, at least I still got you!

WHO'S THE DADDY?

Well on 1st may 2003 I had a little boy Damien he was born at 36 weeks I luckily had no issues at all during this pregnancy unlike the previous two and Damien again by caesarean section as I could not give birth naturally even though I wished to, Damien was born weighing 5lbs, I remember my mum visiting not long afterwards and almost shoving Barry out the door of the hospital room and telling him to go get her a drink, he did as he was told he adored if not worshipped my mum and always listened to what she said, my mum is only person he listened too I still to this day believe he fancied her anyhow first thing my mum said to me was OH MY GOD! I replied to her and simply said what? My mum then said he's got ginger hair he's Liam's isn't he? I said Yes I think so mum and you didn't have push Barry out the door he already knows and I explained everything we'd discussed to her and she smiled said good girl!

Upon leaving hospital I told Liam about the baby birth was literally maybe a few days after leaving the hospital and took Damien to meet him and I even told Barry that Liam may be the father and has a right to see his baby and off I went, Liam made it clear he did not want to know Damien and again said it was best if Barry raised him as his own, That was it then I was stuck I mean I was 21 and had 3 young children aged 4 years, 3 years and a newborn at home and was financially liable and paying for Dean aged 5 who was still living with my mum there was no way I could manage by myself I was constantly tired as it was and skint. I don't know how but I got through the next few years and felt lower than ever, No friends, no energy and was asleep whenever my babies were. I was struggling badly and had no support at all, It looked like I had support from my mum, Hazel and Barry but I didn't which I hope to you is clear by now, again I felt trapped, I was too scared to attempt to seek help outside the family!

Life continued like this for many years then in 2006 trouble seemed to start on the street I lived, I do not know why but it seemed I was suddenly hated. I'd go out with my children to my car and I would get abuse thrown at me, One time I took my kids to get an ice cream and had to walk past this gang of 30 odd year old women and one of them named Angie decided to start mouthing at me I cannot remember why or what happened exactly but next thing I knew my mum was out on the street as she often called round after school and she started grabbing the kids ushering them inside Barry was out in street going round and round in circles shouting and foaming at the mouth saying don't hurt her I'll F'in kill you to which point I turned back around towards Angie and found I had an Air rifle pointed at me by this man I had never seen until now, well me being me and used to being hurt I thought nothing of the danger I was in as I'd already had years of abuse nothing really scared me these days, I was starting to toughen up quite a lot so I turned and strolled quite quickly up to the person and I grabbed the gun by the barrel and pointed it to my head I think it was a shot gun it had two holes and the end? I then went on to say go on then pull the god dam trigger don't just point it at me! To which point the whole gang that was only moments earlier mouthing and laughing all fell silent, turned and looked at me as though I was crazy and with that the guy let go of the gun which I now had hold of by the barrel, He turned around whilst calling me a mad cow and ran into Angies house and all fell silent, I placed the gun near her front gate inside her garden and simply walked up the street 4 doors up and into my home, My kids were in back garden playing unaware of what had just happened, so I simply put kettle on had a cuppa (cup of tea in Yorkshire) and thought no more of it and carried on as normal for rest of the evening and it was pretty much peaceful for rest of evening, well until the next morning any how when I went to take my children to school at 8.30am and noticed my car had a nice shattered windscreen upon closer inspection I could see it was clearly a bullet hole and inside my car on the seat a bullet, I took my kids to school, came back and I rang police who gave me a crime reference number and surprisingly did nothing more about the incident so I got it repaired and again just carried on as did the abuse verbally from the neighbours and harassment it was ridiculous these were other mothers, 10 years my senior mostly easily ... they should be setting an example in front their kids and acting like adults not kids in a playground who don't know better, I was shocked. At this point I was only roughly 25 years old, I remained at this house on Lawrence Street, Grimsby for 2 more years, I had no way of going any were else, the neighbours hated me, I mean looking back I don't blame them I would have hated me too, well possibly not hate and certainly I'd not have treat my neighbours the way these was treating me but I would certainly not have wanted our family as neighbours either that is for sure! Barry caused trouble with the neighbours even though I never knew this at the time later found this out and he shouted at me in the street, he shouted at the kids a lot too and treat us all bad like he'd always done but to me, this was perfectly normal behaviour, I mean my mum had told me everyone argues and that's just what happens she told me this repeatedly time after time when her and Hazel had argued when I was younger so how was I to know any differently? My mum and Hazel had argued with each other and with me all my life, I was told to make Barry happy and to do whatever that took to do so how could him shouting at me and treating us all like this be wrong? No, I had obviously done something as usual to deserve it or he'd not be like this right, I mean my mum & Hazel both told me it was my fault when they treat me how they did so clearly this is just the same? So in that case why were the neighbours acting so nasty towards us if this was such a normal loving adult relationship and behaviour in adulthood? I was sooo confused, I might have been 25 but often I felt dumb, like I knew nothing about the world we lived in, I didn't even know who our Prime Minister was, or how to vote, or even that I had to vote, I got into trouble with TV licence as again I didn't realise I needed one all these years I'd not known! Barry was buying things on credit from different catalogues in both our names making me fill paperwork in as he could not read or write, I refused said we can't afford it he started yelling etc., I learnt just to do as asked simply put, he ran up huge debts totalling thousands of pounds, we was in a mess big style, something had to change, I HAD to change!

ENOUGH IS ENOUGH!

Well in January 2009 I finally started talking to people, The other mothers at the school gates mainly and 1 of them who I spoke to each day for a good few month's must have noticed how run down I was as at first she just started with odd question, then she out right asked me one day if I was ok as she was worried about me and everything came out about how I felt, how my life was and how it had been, we had been stood there after taking our kids in by this time almost 2 hours and she looked horrified, I asked her why she looked so and she told me it was horrible and so very wrong and she advised me I needed to get out of the abusive relationship I laughed and said I'm not in an abusive relationship I seriously did not for 1 minute think I was, I told her I must go as he didn't know where I was and he'd go nuts and she gave me this knowing look, I got home said I am so….. before I could finish my sentence Barry got up from his PC desk, walked towards me, Grabbed me and told me if I was ever late or didn't inform him were I was or was going to and not back in the time I said I would be he wouldn't just stop at this and I again at that moment sunk back into myself and confidence I had got suddenly in that moment …gone, but worse still my friends words stung in my head!

I sat night after night after that and thought about what she'd said and I realised she was indeed very much right, I was in an abusive relationship around this time because I felt so incredibly lonely I was also talking to 'friends' in a chat room on-line one person especially a man called Andre from Australia I talked to him for hours everyone thought there was something between us but I didn't want that I had enough to cope with already he was studying to be a shrink in Australia so he was a good listener but he advised me I needed to get out and do so quickly, This took some planning! I still to this day do not know why Andre was different or why I felt his advice and words were gold but I did and he explained things to me, what adult life should be like, What love was, and how I should be treated, I spent many an hour crying while talking to him this caused major arguments between Barry and I but I suddenly did not care, I realised for the first time in my life I felt the only thing that mattered was the voice in my head screaming at me to get a grip and get the hell out. So I started saving up at first just a few quid a week, I hid money in an old washing powder box in a plastic tub and put washing powder on top of it, he never ever did any housework at all so was no way he'd find it their! I still suspected Barry was talking to women online and now I needed evidence as I was planning on leaving him and getting a divorce and I'd learnt how to use internet and I knew by researching that I needed evidence to prove adultery so I set about obtaining this, I'd make him a coffee take it through to him to look at his pc screen to see what he was doing, i noticed he'd always quickly close the window well minimize it, one day i grabbed mouse and opened it, his face went white, there in a window was a girl of around 17ish, i just walked out the room, she was dressed as he was but i felt sick... a KID!

I mentioned this to my friends they suggested to me a word called grooming, I said no I was not aware of that and they explained it to me in great detail, I felt sick they then said Emma we all think he groomed you, I felt so sick I ran toilet and threw up, I mean yes he has raped me multiple times and what now i was too old for him, he was looking for another younger girl, another victim? I returned back to my PC and returned back to the chat group and even though I think deep down I knew and I felt physically sick I got back on the webcam and microphone and proceeded to say No you're wrong... he didn't, I mean I wasn't...... No your wrong and I left the chat room.

I couldn't shake that conversation out of my mind though and over the next few weeks I caught Barry speaking to more and more teenage girls online, they also some of them looked very young though I was worried at just how young and innocent, Barry swore they was all above 16 and he was only speaking to them anyway so was doing nothing wrong, I still felt sick and worried about my own daughter as well as these other girls too, I knew I had escape ASAP or kill him it was that simple.

I told my uncle my thoughts and he told me not to do anything stupid and to think of my kids if I ended up in prison they'd then be stuck with him with no escape, He was right, I told him not to tell my mum, he agreed and also helped me out greatly and he started helping me look for a place near him in Stanford, I was so grateful for his help, I felt less alone in all this mess.

In the meantime unfortunately turned out to be a good few month's Barry got more and more aggressive, I was now starting to stand up for myself no longer scared but repulsed by this pervert I was forced to live with and who I wanted dead! I and Barry had some blazing rows, I'm ashamed to say often around the kids, I did so try to keep it away from them but Barry wouldn't care where we was, In car, In street, In shop anywhere if he wanted to argue or hit me he would do! Barry one day decided to start yelling at me as usual and Katie appeared she was only roughly 4 or 5 years old bless her but she stood her ground and shouted at her dad, Leave my mummy alone you big bully and why don't you just leave! I was sooo proud of her, but knew Barry wouldn't take kindly to this and before I could react he'd grabbed Katie and slapped her very hard around her bare leg! She only had her undies on as she was upstairs before this time getting changed out of her school uniform, I grabbed Katie shoved her behind me shouted others downstairs and told them all to go to Sheba our Alsatian which I knew would protect them and stay with her in the kitchen! I thumped Barry and rang the police, I told the police they had better hurry up and come as I was going into kitchen once I had put phone down and if Barry came after us I would stab him! He was still shouting at this point and saying look what you made me do now, saying I had to not press charges or he'd kill me etc. etc. The police arrived and took him away in a riot van!

I honestly thought that was it, end of it all and was so relieved, I never for one second thought they would just caution him and let him return home, In fact they actually brought him home, explaining how cause his mental health issues I was his appointee as his wife and legally responsible for him... WHAT! I told them I was leaving him and I'd stab him in the night if he stayed there, they told me well then you'll face murder charges so we advise you don't! They then left, he looked smugly at me and said I'm going nowhere! I actually started thinking up ways of killing him so I could get away with it and make it look like a burglary gone wrong or something..... It happens right

MY NEW BEGINNING!

I n June 2009 my uncle Edward managed to find me a house to rent in Stanford, Doncaster, I told Barry we needed a new start and got him to move all our belongings while the kids were at school, we never told my mum nor the kids or anything I knew my mum wouldn't approve, as expected upon telling my mum she took the news of us moving very badly, she tried threatening me, she tried saying I would not cope you name it she tried it but my mind was made up, I did lie though to my mum and Barry I said it was a fresh start and how much we needed this to stay together, I only told my nanna and Uncle the truth which was my real plans... To put Tenancy agreement in only my name... which I did....to let Barry move in with me then on day of first argument I could say you have not changed, This aint a fresh start this is exactly the same shit...get out!

We moved in on 3rd June 2009 and on 9th June 2009, we had that argument with Barry starting it sort of hahaha... Ok I admit I caused most of it but I was fed of waiting for him he seemed to be actually trying but by this point I wasn't interested to be honest I had now realised I never actually ever was, I just wanted a way out of the abuse I was suffering daily at home and that seemed a better way out than be dead by killing myself or living with daily hell and abuse, ah if only I had known this was much worse abuse than ever before and I now realised I was abused, I had been raped, I had been groomed I hated Barry he made me angry and feel sick his smile repulsed me, anyhow I was ill and I had asked him to keep an eye on the kids while

I grabbed a hours sleep on the sofa, he let them out to play and woke me up not long after I had fell to sleep to say he could not find Damien, I'd strictly told him not to let the kids out in back garden as it was unsafe at moment, It needed the old furniture the previous tenants had left dumped their a freezer, a sofa and lots other metal sharp bits and very long waist high thick reed type of grass and nettle's sorting out, I was fuming and worried and flew out to the back garden, none of kids was their! I ran to the side gate it was open, I ran into street shouting their names, I found Damien and the other 2 out the front of the house on the street playing with the other neighbours kids, luckily only a side street but none the less I was not amused as the side street led to a very busy 40 road that led to a national speed limit road and all the cars sped past our road top at way past 40 mph it was not safe at all, Rory was 8, Katie 7 and Damien only just turned 5 years old, what the hell did Barry think he was doing the other neighbours said aww they'll be ok but I didn't feel they was so I got my kids back inside, I mean I didn't even know these people so I couldn't trust them with my kids, I knew liars and monsters existed now and no one was hurting my babies EVER!

Upon getting my children back inside the house I asked them to go their rooms and watch a dvd please whilst I had words with Daddy, I went mental at Barry something inside me had snapped I do not know how or what happened but for the first time in years I felt strong and threw Barry out, Lithely I grabbed hold of him by the shoulders, opened my front door and pushed him out the door he stumbled and fell of the two steps that led up to my front door, I told him we needed space even though I knew I meant we were finished but I also knew if I told Barry this he'd never leave! He stood outside in front garden yelling about his pc and how he wanted his PC and was not leaving without it... His PC all he was bothered about says a lot doesn't it!

I closed front door, all the time he is yelling stuff and I'm laughing, I went upstairs, opened bedroom window and threw his tower out of it... somehow he caught it I honestly even now am impressed by that I think it's the only time he ever did impress me hahaha! I soon threw the rest of his belongings out too, First his PC screen, followed by all his clothes 1 item at a time, My god it felt great then lastly the black bags for him to pack his stuff into...oh how I made sure I got him to look up for that shot and it worked as he looked up I threw the black bags which hit him directly in the face, now that felt great the look on his face, I recall me laughing and him saying to me in a pathetic voice how will he get all his stuff to his mums as he has no credit and no money etc. I said don't worry I'll gladly ring and pay for the Taxi which I did and surprisingly he just left..... Peacefully!

Barry went to his mothers in Skellow and life settled into a routine Monday to Friday I would have the children and take them to school, bath them do the normal day to day things, you know the stuff homework, Tea, Play time, Bath, Supper, Bed and repeat this was my weekday routine whilst kids at school I'd do housework and try to get much unpacking done as possible but it wasn't easy as for some reason last few week I had started feeling so tired, I would take kids to school then do 1 household chore sit down with a cuppa, watch a tv program and next thing my alarm would be going off to say it was time to get kids a full day was passing and I have got nothing done, It was ridiculous I had no support, My Nanna, My uncle all my family I suddenly realised had only visited the once since I'd kicked Barry out....I had been that busy, That tired I had not even realised, nor made any effort either in any way to contact them, I'd simply just been too tired to think, I guess I was thinking back acting on autopilot, functioning but not really thinking right, possibly was the start of what I later found out was a mental breakdown, On a Saturday the kids would spend the day with Barry as since me leaving him he had gone Drs and got on medication for his temper and had actually calmed down, seemed happier, accepted we was over and was really trying so I agreed he could see the children so long as his mum was there to start with and go from there, this worked out for a short while a few weeks maybe, but the kids begged to see their dad more telling me they missed him, he was there daddy and they had a right and they hated me, it was horrible and he too wanted the same, I must admit the kids seemed happy and me and Barry were getting along and when Barry mentioned him having them Friday night til Sunday I agreed but his mum expressed that there were no way Barry could have the children staying over at hers due to it being a 3 bedroom house and there was Barry and his brother both back at home after failed relationships, both their kids visited on a weekend and Susan was in her words getting on and it was getting too much as things was and needed to change, How I had a house so why didn't Barry stay there and I go out somewhere and rest, she felt Barry was able to have the children by himself now mentally too, so I had a solution I'd met a guy called Kev who lived at Nottingham and I wanted to go visit him, so I agreed to Susan's idea and that evening I explained things to the kids how that there dad was going to come on a Friday evening and sleep at ours, look after them and have fun until Sunday afternoon when I would return and daddy would then go back to his mummies house where he lived, They hugged me and said thank you all 3 seemed very happy, I really wasn't happy, To be honest I still wanted my kids nowhere near him, but he was their dad and he had changed since been on the meds the more I thought about it, the more perfect it seemed as I was tired and it meant I got time to myself as I was struggling looking after a 3 young children 1 of which was mentally disabled and didn't sleep well at night, It gave me the welcome break I needed so I could care better for my kids during the week and be the best mum to them I could possibly be!

Things went great for a good month or so, the kids reported to me upon my return what they had done, each Friday I gave Barry as much as I had spare often was between £50 and £100 so he could take kids out, he couldn't cook so it was also money for him to go chip shop, or order a takeaway etc. and to take them swimming or somewhere on a Saturday and upon my return the kids would tell me what they'd done, Barry would leave, never giving me any change obviously times I asked he reckoned he'd spent it all so I never asked again, but in July 2009 things changed yet again for the worse.

The social workers got involved in my life, I don't remember the reason why to be honest I wasn't even told why at the start, all I was told is don't leave Barry with the children alone! Now I thought ok fair doo's, easier said than done the kids screamed and screamed and wanted to see their dad each day they'd be so upset asking to see their daddy, I caved in and allowed this to happen and I went to Nottingham to visit Kev leaving Barry with the children as I used to do on a Friday evening the kids were sooo very happy and I felt 1 weekend wouldn't hurt would it? Barry did not know where I was going or doing but had my number in case of emergencies, well somehow Barry found out where I was and what I was doing, he rang me up while I was at Kev's, I had only just arrived only a 1 hr. A 40-minute drive from where I lived. I was already angry and upset as my car had broken down and it was late Friday evening and garage where I was said he could not get part needed to fix it until Monday I was supposed to be home on Sunday and I only had £20 the cost of the part left and did not get paid until Monday as I had given my last £50 to Barry for the children for him to take them out over the weekend like I always did which left me with fuel and £20 left. I explained this to Barry to which he started shouting at me and saying I'd better get my F***ing ass home as if I didn't get home in a hour he were going to dump the kids and leave them alone! I thought he was being stupid and making his usual idle threats as he's always said I'll do this and I'll do that when in one of his rants but never did do anything he threatened, I knew

Barry made threats we were safe it was when he was quiet that we were to worry the most, how very wrong was I! He rang my mum who rushed through from Grimsby to Doncaster and collected my children for me she was to watch them until I got back on Monday. Come Monday I rang my mum to arrange to go collect the children to which she told me she was not allowed to do so, She asked me if I had yet got home, I informed her I was only just setting off from having car repaired and I was going home to drop off some items then I'd be straight through to hers after I had called at cash machine as I'd only just got paid today. My mum then informed me she was instructed by the social workers to not let me take my children and that she was to look after them until further notice. I was fuming, in tears and to be honest shock, I didn't know if this was true and if so why? I drove home fast too fast and within the hour was pulling into my drive.

THE AWFUL TRUTH

I got home to find a letter from social services asking me to ring them upon me receiving the letter as a matter of urgency and <u>NOT</u> to go through to my mum's or try to collect the children until doing so! I rang the number and the lady that answered took my details and then informed me there would be a social worker out within the hour, I sat there shaking and crying, The social worker came out to see me and explained there was an issue and stated that as I know because I was asked to not leave the children with Barry previously and had done so they asked me why did I do so? I stated I had asked what the reason was I couldn't leave Barry with his own kids, has I had previously already done in the past but this time I demanded I was told the truth, it was then I was told the sick truth that reminded me of those video chats years ago I'd long forgot about.....Barry been reported for having a naked photo of Katie and was showing it to a neighbour of mine and asking if he wanted to purchase it for £5!

Obviously, I went nuts at not being told this before when I had asked has if I had of been informed I would never have left the kids with him again supervised never mind alone, I ran to bathroom and threw up, I returned said ok I agree obviously, now what? I was then told if I wanted any chance of getting my children back it was in my interests to work with the social workers and do as they say, I obviously agreed to work with them and do anything they requested I do, I was in a complete mess, for numerous reasons the most obvious one being that I'd left my babies with such a monster even if was unknowingly and secondly my heart was being torn apart that I could not have them with me right away as she'd just explained and went on to say more, My mind was buzzing at this point, I had so much rushing through it, questions, anger, yelling at myself, calling myself stupid etc. etc. she was still speaking but I wasn't aware what she was saying i felt strange......My head was spinning, I felt all hot, then cold, I was shaking and feeling really unwell and lightheaded at this point as well as being so dammed angry that I was never told up to this point why I should never leave kids with Barry alone, In my eye's how I saw it I'd never have let him within 100 feet of them if I had been told.

The social worker Daniel said Emma are you listening to me this is serious! I snapped back to reality and said sorry yes go on.... Daniel then stated they'd be out soon to do an assessment and told me to sign a form I can't recall what it was but stating that I agreed for my kids to stay with my mum in her care temporarily, I had no option but to agree and sign it as I was told if I didn't they'd take me to court and get the papers which would go against me in the long term as they said it'd look like I was uncooperative and difficult.

That next week was a living nightmare for me, I thought my life was bad before now I knew what hell was, I went to Kev's as just couldn't stay in my family home without my children it was far too painful, I got a phone call a week later and returned home to meet the social worker, Kev came with me for support and the social worker asked who it was, I replied my friend Kev from Nottingham a guy I was casually seeing if you can call it that it was more a friendship than owt else, whoops big mistake she then laid into me about casually seeing a guy when I should've been there for my children, I stated I was always there for my children etc. etc. Anyhow she assessed the house I live in and wrote up a huge list that needed doing, I asked her when my kids could come back and her reply was as soon as this is done we will come to check then they can be returned to you, The list was such pathetic things e.g.: Garden to be made safe and secure for children to play in, the long reed grass right down bottom of my 25ft garden (10 foot was high and was not taken care off in many years and had until recently been fenced off I took fence down to do the garden when we first moved in to make it better for my kids) Grass To be cut, New bed for Damien as his was broken as he used it as a trampoline as kids do.. 3rd bed in a few months (I had already planned to purchase one the week they got taken off me anyhow) and house to be decorated and lots other really pathetic things like unpack rest of boxes I'd not yet fully unpacked!

I agreed to do this list and Kev offered to come to live with me temporarily til I had done the list so he could help me, he lived with his mum, didn't work etc. so I agreed and he asked his friend to also come and help too, I thought why heck not the more hands the better right? Well within 2 week's we had done everything on the list and more, I had not heard any more from the social workers so I rang them, it took me another 2 weeks before I got through to right person as they kept saying oh we'll ring you back, I went into office was told nobody to speak to etc. I by this time felt like giving up on life the only thing that kept me going was getting my babies back. It turns out this was not going to be as straight forward as previously thought, I still at this point was none the wiser to what exactly was happening, I didn't know what time it was or what day it was, never mind the month I sank into a world of all new low If I thought things were bad before I was very, very wrong!

MEETING WITH THE SOCIAL WORKER FROM HELL!

When I finally had a meeting with the social worker it wasn't one I knew it was an older woman with a bad attitude who told me she wasn't my social worker, I wasn't getting kids back, that I would not be assigned a social worker as I didn't need one, she was my kids social worker and acted for them, I was told there was more to the case they yet could not tell me, I can't explain what was running through my mind at this time, but I knew I wanted and deserved some answer's, I asked if I could go get my children and was told they did not wish me to do so??? I was then informed only Damien wished me to collect him and that I could do so, Obviously I rang my mum and collected him that night, We sat cuddled up on the sofa and I thought I would never ever let him go ever again, Damien asked me if he would be taken again and I said no baby I won't let that happen, your home now and you're staying here, He said mummy can we just run away, I cried and told him we couldn't do that and I promised him he was staying with me as I thought this to be true. The very next morning I received a phone call from another social worker asking why I had gone and collected Damien when I was instructed not to and signed paperwork agreeing to children being with my mum until court date I said I was told I could do so I even had a text to prove it as I texted Daniel to state I had collected Damien and thanking her and she text back saying good you two be safe and others shall be back with you soon. The social worker 'Lara then stated that this should never have happened and they were coming to collect Damien immediately, I told them no way, I hung up and rang my nanna who came straight round, I was a mess suddenly again I felt like that terrified little girl many, many years ago, My nanna was obviously furious too and 20 minutes later the social workers arrived Damien was already crying and upset at this point as I explained to him he might have to go back to his nanna's again and he didn't wish to do so, The social worker told me it was best if I take him to the car of my own free will and tell Damien it is ok he will be back soon it just a holiday, So I did was I was instructed as was told if they had to remove him by force they would do so and I didn't want my poor baby seeing that, I put him in the car that was parked at end of my road and they drove off, I broke down hit the floor and do not remember anything else after that apart from my nanna carrying me with Kev back into my home. I then had a call days later stating that I was under investigation for child neglect and abuse, but no further details were given only that I should seek a solicitor I did so and they really wasn't a great help at all they just seemed to agree with everything the social worker says, so I presumed if these solicitors stood no chance what hope did I really have, The social workers did a background check on me and Kev which I was fine with me I had never even been questioned by police before so I knew I had a clean record but that night when I got home from solicitors and informed Kev his face went white I asked him what was the matter and he said he'd been in trouble before for ABH, GBH and other stuff, I now was scared Kev too had a temper I'd recently seen after requesting he moved out and he refused telling me he was living there and while I was ill he had gone to jobcentre and made a claim as a couple with another woman he'd said was ME! I can go on to say I was fuming but I really wasn't I didn't care nothing mattered any more, my babies were gone, my heart ripped out.

It is now end of September 2009 it feels like it has been years but it has only been 2 months, I heard a rumour that Kev was hiding something from me, and cheating on me, He was always out but I didn't care about him, or about my life or anything really at that point but did want to know what he was hiding so while he was out one day I searched through his stuff and remembered about some CD's he'd told me to never ever touch, Oh how I wish I hadn't I inserted one onto his PC and found the imagines appearing on screen I ran to the bathroom and was violently sick, I'd only gone and let a flipping pedo in my home!

MY DEALINGS WITH THE POLICE

I obviously immediately went to the police station at Doncaster and asked to speak to an officer regarding my findings, I was interviewed by DCI Moonie a child and family law Inspector or something like that and after taking a statement from me he said he'd like to collect the computer that also belonged to Kev, I of cause agreed and asked him to also remove Kev from my home as I was scared of what he'd do to me if he knew I'd gone police, He said Kev would not find out I had grassed him up. I trusted Moonie and thought if you can't trust the police who can you trust, DCI Moonie drove me home and collected the desktop at same time, a little while later a police car appeared out front of my home and they arrested Kev, I breathed a sigh of relief as soon as they had left my home, That was short lived though as the very next morning at 7 am I received a phone call from Kev stating he was on his way home, 5 minutes later a call from Moonie stating I was to allow him to stay with me until they had further evidence as if Kev were to return to Nottingham they'd not be able to arrest or charge him, I felt powerless I did not want this sicko in my house but also I wanted Kev to be charged and off the streets so no other kids could ever be hurt, To look at Kev when he walked through that front door was dam hard work never mind act normal, Kev guessed it was me and he was fuming I ran up to my room where I had left my phone to ring the police, He grabbed me threw me on the bed and put a knife to my throat, I didn't feel scared or fearful in fact I hoped he'd do it as what did I have to live for? He said if I screamed he'd kill me so I screamed and

97

you guessed it he never did anything just shouted n shouted, I don't know how long he kept me pinned for with the knife to my throat but it seemed like hours, Eventually he released me and I kicked him hard in his lower religion, grabbed my phone he had threw across the room and ran downstairs locked myself in bathroom and called police, He didn't even bother to come downstairs, I only answered door when they said officers were outside, I ran to the front door just as the officers entered the house and showed them the marks and were Kev was, I felt safe now thought surely they'll keep him away from me, but that next morning yet again I was proved wrong and they released him due to lack of evidence!!!

So the nightmare continues, Kev returned yet again back to my home and stated if I ever pulled a trick like that again he would go through to my mum's snatch my kids from their schools and he came out with their school names, that he'd kill them in front of me then let me live so I was tortured the rest of my life!

He knew I did not care for my life but how much my babies meant to me and I believed he was capable too! So I let him stay and did what the police and him requested, In November 2009 Kev was yet again arrested, The police informed me the form I'd signed meant the social workers was taking me to court for a finding of facts hearing and I'd hear from them soon as my mum was going for special guardianship order for the care of my children.... WHAT!

I didn't know what to say or believe, That night I received a phone call I do not know who from but it was a man and he went on to state my home was going to be fire bombed that very night with me in it, I believed with all my heart this would happen, so I started loading my car up with all I could fit in it, My case of clothes, My paperwork from social services, TV, computer, Photographs of kids, Box of kids certificates etc. etc. I only had a little Vauxhall Corsa and was shocked at how much I could get into it. I drove to the only place I could go to which was my friends Ant's In Margate, Kent over 300 miles away, I arrived there at   3 am in the morning, and there I stayed for almost 2 month's I knew by this time I was not going to get my kids back, I was now homeless and the court had issued my mum a legal document stating kids should stay with her until the case is over which could take month to years, the form was called an interim care order.

I had come to learn life really could get worse, a lot worse I always thought living with a manic depressive and sexual predator as a husband was bad enough then I found out it could get worse, Honestly my childhood, living with my mum, The abuse all of it I'd go back to it IF it meant not being away from me babies! My god I would give anything to have that life back if it meant my children were with me, that pain was nothing compared to this I was feeling now, well apart from the husband bit I'd not take him back if he was the last man on earth and the future depended upon us breeding! There are certain limits and lows one just should not sink too and he is one of those lows!

LIFE TAKES ON A WHOLE NEW LOW!

Well it's now November 2009 I have had death threats, been told I if I ever return to Stanford I would be killed, had threats online, Threats and names called everywhere saying I was scum, dead, how could I do that and must be true as her own mother said so etc. etc. but not one person ever told me what it was that my mum was saying and to top it all my mum informs me my children now do not wish to speak to me on the phone no longer and as it there wish she has to listen to what they want, but the way she said it so coldly and sharp makes me think who is this person, where has the kind hearted warm mum I once knew gone, It was then at that moment I had my eye's opened for me which resulted in a terrible breakdown for me, I went off the rails completely I don't remember a thing from end Sep to end Nov apart from one night Ant and his friend decided they were going out clubbing and I should go with them to 'cheer me up' I thought whatever at least I can drown my sorrows, Well as I was getting ready Ant's friend 'Chucky' came into the bedroom and offered me this little white thing wrapped in cling film, I asked her what it was and her reply was it'll take your mind off things for tonight and let you have a good time! I knew it was some type of drug but thought what the hell, I have nothing to live for so I may as well so I popped this tiny thing into my mouth and swallowed, We all went out to this club in Margate I remember buying drink after drink but didn't feel at all any different, I told Chucky and she told me to follow her to toilet and told me to take another this one was a bit bigger, I still felt no different and an hour later we went home. I don't remember getting home or in bed but I remember the next morning waking up, lifting my head off the pillow and it feeling like a lead brick, I stood up and my whole body ached so badly, I dragged myself into the living room and whimpered morning to Ant and Mark, Mark laughed and told Ant he'd better sort me out I grunted that I was just going lay down on sofa a bit, Ant came in with another wrapped white thing and told me it was only way to take the pain away or sweat it out my choice, I told him no thanks I do not think so, I instantly knew at that moment I did want to live and didn't wish to stay there any longer but I knew first I needed to get control back of my life and my body!

◆ ◆ ◆

Well 2 weeks later I decided now was right time to look for somewhere else to live, I waited until Ant had gone out with Mark and I logged onto his pc and started searching for a place to live, I didn't care what type place so long as was back near my children in Grimsby, I found a number for a room to let and rang it up, the lady stated I could go look at it the very next day, I explained I was travelling from Margate and could only travel to view room if she was defiantly going to let me have it, The lady at first was unsure until I explained my circumstances and then the lady called Linda agreed. I immediately started packing my car up with my belonging's and upon Ant's arrival he asked me what I was doing, so I told him leaving and that he'd better have the £450 he owed me, Ant stated he only had £250 but I'd been there long enough to know he got his disability money the next day so I told him in morning we are going to cash machine and you will give me my goddam money! Well, 9 am the next day I did as I stated drove Ant kicking n screaming that he'd not got it to cash machine, at first he made out he'd not got his card followed by oh I forgot my pin but as soon as I stated ok let's go into the bank he soon remembered it and to my astonishment he had £759 in his account but I could see that £479 was his rent benefit so I told him to look give me £400 and we'll forget about the other £50, He obviously put up some fuss but eventually handed over the cash to me and moaned about doing so all way back to his.

NEW STARTS

Well I settled in nicely to the room I was letting it was in a huge house in Cleethorpes, it had an old 'ish couple as the landlords Fred & Linda they used to be foster parents until Fred's accident that left him in a wheelchair, and Linda now worked in adult social services in Doncaster, In the house was 1 other tenant an old guy called Rob in the room next to mine and the only other person in this huge house was the landlords son who you never ever saw he seemed to live in his room all day and night! The house was quite big it had 3 floors, first floor had a tenants Livingroom, a kitchen to back and a backyard, second floor had my room to the back a nice sized room with 3 fitted wardrobes in it but 2 was full of quilts and pillows etc., a dressing table, a bed and a set of draws and 2 windows, Then there was old man's room a tiny single room next to mine and landlords opposite mine, Upstairs was their sons room and the Attic which was a games room it had a pool table and big soft comfy sofa's all way round the room and was brightly decorated I felt calm in there and often just went in there to sit and let my mind drift and listen to music with my headphones on.

I stayed in this house for a few week's but after Christmas, they started trying to be my parent's telling me I could have friends over but certainly No guys and I could only have a 'Man' friend over if I introduced him to them first, I told them I was not dating/ seeing anyone and that was an issue as most my friends are male but they swore blind they'd heard me having sex which I certainly had NOT! I only wish I had, I mean I was fed of being lonely and bored and without company, it was depressing, New year's eve arrived and I decided I was going to go out alone for a few drinks, Walking down the street a guy across the road whistled then disappeared into a taxi,,,, He was quite fit...typical, A few hours later at 1am I walked home, It was snowing, I was freezing but had a good night.

Having being controlled in my life before I certainly was not going to let anyone control me ever again, so I yet again set out looking for another room to let I mean I was 27 Years old I really did not wish to be treat like a teen again, I stumbled upon a website that offered many rooms to let in a shared house, one advert caught my eye and I rang about it and a man named Peter stated I could look around that very day, I met Peter at 3 pm got the key's and moved in that same day, This was much better house, The other residents were nice there was Zack, Louise and her boyfriend and a foreign couple, The foreign couple soon moved out did a midnight flit took all of Peter's furniture with them and left owing Peter money too!

I started looking for work and had a fair few interviews lined up a barmaid & a canvassing job which was a start for first week, I attended the bar staff job interview first and was shocked at what the interview entailed, there was 12 of us and we were each asked what our party trick was, Now as I previously explained I did not ever attend parties, being a teen mum I didn't get to experience life as many do, so I informed them I couldn't really do anything and felt quite embarrassed at the way they looked at me like how can you not know a party trick, if I am honest I was not even sure what classed as a party trick, next we were split into 2 groups and told we had 10 minutes to coronagraph a dance routine, my group found this really unfair as the other team had a professional dancer in it and we all in our group honestly didn't have a clue where to start none of us really knew how to put a dance together we all looked at each other, we gave it our best shot and to say we were useless would be an understatement but I shocked myself when I stood forward and spoke up saying if we did this and took charge, the other groups performance put us to shame big style, to say they was awesome would be an understatement and I left the interview feeling more withdrawn and with less confidence in myself than I felt previously!

On the second interview I was extremely nervous but by this time had learnt to hide it well and used fake confidence, So I plastered a smile on my face and hid my big black puffy eyes with plenty of makeup which I applied in my car just before going in so it looked fresh as it could, I got speaking to the other interviewees and my nerves started to ease a little, this didn't last long though as the two men holding the interviews arrived and all I could think was... WOWZERS! One of them was sooooo very handsome and on second glance I realized it was the guy that had shouted hello to me on New Year's Eve but at that time he was drunk, his friend had dragged him into the waiting taxi saying I was too good for him and out of his league and the taxi drove off! I couldn't take my eyes off this sexy guy stood in front of me, Lee the other guy was chatting about the job and money and what it entailed etc. I should have been listening to these details more but I was transfixed, I'd never ever felt like this before and I was mesmerized, here's this guy I'd never spoken to or knew but had these feeling's I didn't understand but quite liked growing in me it felt like butterflies were dancing in my stomach, I felt giddy and all shy, My cheeks felt flushed, I found out his name was James! Aaaahhhh James what a sexy name with his dark hair and chiselled jaw and WOW those sexy blue eyes and those lips omg those lips so Shapley and just begging to be kissed, I suddenly heard Lee say Emma so I snapped out of it and apologised to which he asked me to say a bit about myself, I stood up looked at James and in the very first sentence declared I was single!

I didn't only get the job I got promoted to the team leader that very same day and got a lager and burger meal bought for me too I have a feeling this is going to be a good job in many ways!

A week later I went to pick James up in my car and we went out canvassing together, I asked him if there was any significant other in his life to which he blushed and said no not for a good few years now at all, I said what? A nice guy like you single no way! I caught James giving me the eye a few times but I couldn't believe this guy who looked like he belonged in a modelling agency would ever look twice at plain looking average if that little flat chested me, with his looks he could have his choice of women I was sure never mind with his sweet, kind caring personality too, My feelings just grew and grew over those next few weeks and I realized I was falling for my boss big style this was the very first time I'd actually fallen for a guy, I decided it was best if I quit so I called James and explained he sounded upset and asked me to deliver the flyers to him, upon arrival James came out and my god my stomach did summersaults, this was the first time I'd seen James out of a suit and he had this beige jumper on and blue jeans he looked dam good! James got into my car and I realised he smelt just as good as he looked too, we got chatting and I decided to test the water, I reached across to the glove box and as I did so I brushed my hand on James knee and looked into his eyes whilst doing so, he gasped slightly which was all I needed to know I maybe did stand a chance after all so I took a deep breath and I told him why I was quitting, cause I had fallen for the boss he looked at me said Liam he has a girlfriend, I said No you, how can we work together when I fancy you, I bottled up the courage and asked James out for a drink, He accepted and upon getting out of car said it's a date, YEESSSSSS-SSSSSS !!!!!!!!!!!!!!!!!!!!

◆ ◆ ◆

Well I spoke to James a lot on an online chat program over those next few days and we texted a lot, I couldn't wait until Saturday to see him so I suggested moving the date to Thursday evening instead and James agreed, I told him I had better go get my stuff I need ready, I didn't own 1 single item that was good enough for a first date, Off I went into Grimsby town it was already 3 pm on Wednesday and I knew I'd be too nervous for shopping the next day, I bought myself a little black skirt and a corset-style top that was tied up at back, and made a little trip into that special adult shop, There I bought some fishnet stockings and some edible chocolate body paint and a set of massage oils, my god what had got into me?

I was a mess mentally and so needed a distraction, a reason to fight, a little bit off happiness so why at same time did I feel so guilty about having a date? It was because truth be told I desperately wanted to be with my children putting them to bed not out being single and acting like I was, I couldn't adapt to this life easily, I was told I should get used to it by the social services as I wasn't getting my kids back, It was that black and white. So really what option did I have but to carry on? Job centre was telling me find a job or lose your benefits, no one cared about my mental state, was it bad or was it all in my head? My god I was confused! HELP ME SOMEONE PLEASE!

MEETING JAMES

Well Thursday evening soon came and I set off in a taxi to meet James, we'd arranged to meet near the seafront, as James approached I saw how sexy he looked and noticed a few of the other women around looking at him, he never even noticed them! He saw me smiled and immediately took his coat off and wrapped it around my shoulders saying, wow you look very nice but must be freezing it was after all 28th January 2010!

We both looked n felt nervous so I bit the bullet and said don't I get a kiss then, James's eye lit up and like a gentleman that he is he leaned in and kissed me on my cheek so sweetly I told him that was sweet but that isn't the kiss I wanted, he then took me by the hips and kissed me on my lips, pulled away saw me grinning and then went on to kiss me more passionately.

We had a great time that night and we needed up back at mine, The next morning I asked James if this meant we were a couple or if it was the start of something special or a 1 off, James replied if you want us to be! James never really left after that we were inseparable and all a sudden life felt and looked brighter, I had a reason to wake in a morning and a reason to live, James rescued me from a life that I had many times I had considered ending and almost a few times had come rather close to doing so.

A few months later I decided I needed to tell James all about my life, what I had been through and was going through as I did so tears welling up James held my hand and listened and gave me a cuddle were needed. James never looked shocked or horrified, he never judged me in fact James helped me see I wasn't to blame and pointed a lot out to me I had not realised and together we tried to fight for my children back but on 7th June 2010 the social services held a court hearing at Sheffield well over a hour away on public transport but James came with me, I wasn't allowed inside the court room, Me and James waited in the waiting area along with lots of other people, all looking as destressed and worried as I, Their James met Barry for first time, Barry upon spotting us started mouthing and pointing then said something to James about me and warning him off me saying I would break his heart etc. etc. It was pathetic but he was spitting and red faced and quite angry pointing his little chubby finger, I sat there and sat Barry shut up your looking like a fool, This other lady stood up from behind me said look mate I am not in mood and I have dealt with little men like you before so I suggest you do one as all us here do not like little men like you! I looked around and quite a few looked angry or upset, I decided it was best If me and James went out for a cig and on way out I informed a security guard what had just happened and upon our return I was informed he was in a side room with a security guard and would remain there until he left.

A few hours later my solicitor came out of the court room and told me she'd be in touch, that my mum had a good chance of getting a special Guardianship order and that the social services had a good strong case against me and we could now leave and she would be in touch, a few days later I was sent a letter, what it stated horrified me to the bone, It still haunts me each night now, I know I am not guilty and was proven as so but It's the fact I was even accused of it in first place that is bad enough, It was the very first time I had EVER seen any accusations or been told of any towards me up to now I was told it was all to do with Barry and because of the incident with the PC and Kev!!

I was horrified as I knew it was utter rubbish, I wasn't the best mum who is, I made plenty of mistakes, but I certainly wasn't neglectful I was abused so I went out my way to make sure my kids wanted for nothing and was fed, looked after, bills paid, holidays and day trips, could swim, ice skate went to clubs socialised with other kids etc.

The court paper stated; The local authority contends that the children concerned have suffered, are likely to suffer, significant harm; and that the harm, or likelihood of harm, is attributable to the care given to the children, or likely to be given to them if the order were not made, not being what it would be reasonable to expect a parent to give him. Inside it then went on to list the accusations raised against me which was;

1. Unacceptable home conditions

2. Prioritising my needs of a partner over children (Kev, Liam, Andre)

3. Allowing Kev to live at her home (Even though was at request of a police officer)

4. Putting kids at risk by allowing unsupervised access to the children by; on one occasion Kev the children's father in spite of his inability to parent

Honest to god I was in total shock! For starters the social services gave me a list of things to do around the home and I did them as requested and the list nor my home was never checked in fact a social worker never came out at all to me after they removed my kids from my home, so how can they put that on, especially since was unfair i no longer lived there to prove my innocence on that side of it, Second one; Prioritising my needs of a man over my kids? Oh my! First Kev was after I'd lost my kids and was nothing more than a friend as previously stated, Andre lived in Australia and was an online friend as I had already told the social worker, and Liam well again years ago way before the case, how unfair! 3rd allegation was at the request of the police and my kids was already at this time living in my mums care and removed from me, so how did this impact on my kids or me for that matter, I was helping snare a criminal... a Peado.... did they think I wanted him in my home, I felt sick when looked at him! Regarding the others Liam was many years ago almost 7 years and Andre was a friend, 4th One Kev read the kids a bed time story 1 evening that was it, the once and only time before I found out what he had done previously etc. and I have already explained Barry and that's the only one I do feel guilt over, I wish I'd listened to my gut when kids asked, begged, cried to see him and said no you can't I'm sorry, instead I put their feelings first, why did I do that?

In September 2011 my mum got awarded a special guardianship of my 3 precious babies', I swear if it wasn't for James holding me up and being there for me and not leaving my side I'd have taken my life that day, Today I feel I owe my life to him I will always be thankful to James for being there.

The courts ruled I could only see my children if they wanted to see me which they didn't so that was left as indirect contact unless the kids stated otherwise which consisted of a letter and a Christmas card, birthday card and present on birthday and xmas that was it, every morning was hell, I felt happy with James but also felt sad like a huge part of me was missing, a huge vacant black hole in my heart I cried often even when something made me smile I cried, when I was angry I cried, when I laughed I cried all I seemed to do was cry I'm surprised James hung around, the Kids birthdays, Christmas Plays, Easter, even hearing a kid laugh or a child shout mummy was complete torture.

I just didn't understand why my life had gone like this, why my babies had been removed from me, I'd take a bullet for any of my kids without thinking it's what we do, we protect our young, why was I kept from mine... Why were they saying they didn't wish to see me when we used to be so close, we'd cuddle and I'd play with them in back garden, I was the type daft mu you'd find bouncing on trampoline with her kids, or chasing them around caravan on holiday having a water fight etc. I have many photos of us all having such fun, so why would my kids say they didn't wish to see me it made no sense to me!

I found out not long after, My uncle informed me my mum had bought them all lots of games, toys and my mum even went as far to buy my kids affections as to buy my older 3 a pony each..... Yes a pony, so long as she was happy with what they said and had to keep saying it and be good and do as they was told or they'd lose it, my uncle said I feel awkward as I can't speak up if I do none of us will know how the kids are, and he was right he was my only way of knowing what really was going off!

There was a lot of upset between my mum and I over the next few months, crossed words and eventually, with all her lies our relationship crumbled totally and we all but had stopped talking, things was totally horrible in one hand and beautiful on the other as somehow through all this disaster and during it James had appeared my very own angel... Still by my side, at the time he helped me see we needed to get a place together, show unity and that we was in a stable loving long term serious relationship and to fight the accusations then there was no reason why I'd not get my kids back, he said he'd stand by me, and he sure did each step, jump and mountain I struggled with James pulled me up and never let me go.

DOWNWARD SPIRAL!

It's now middle 2012 and we've lived in a 3 bedroom maisonette in Grimsby for almost a year now that we obtained from the council but the laws changing, a new tax is coming out and with their just being me & James in a 3 bedroom place we can't afford to stay in our first proper home together, we'd moved in with nothing at all to our names and now we had all the basic household items, All kitchen white items and was doing good but even though we love our home and area and the neighbours were lovely and we called it home, and it was convenient as even though we both held driving licences we couldn't afford a car and our home was so close to the shops and bus station etc. but once the bedroom tax came out we struggled badly and often we was without food and life wasn't easy so we've decided a completely fresh start in Doncaster is on cards, we chose Doncaster as I knew area and was born there and also my mum had moved back to Doncaster in my Aunt Jossalynn house she had rented to my mum in Edington and took my kids a good 50 miles away from me I wasn't impressed at her changing their schooling and uprooting them yet again either, I can't seem to sleep when I do I keep waking, sweating and crying, I can't seem to eat or anything, I felt so depressed, we both sat and decided we were going to start looking at selling everything and moving into a shared house once again... We've done it once, we will again it's just for now and it'd save us money too and mean we can eat right and decrease the stress too... We hope!

RETURNING HOME

Well, it is 2013 we've lived in Doncaster 6 months and we love our area, the Room we rented is on a nice street in a village called Intake, the hospital I was born in is at end of my street how's that for returning home, the house has 2 double rooms downstairs and the kitchen leading out to the back garden and 3 bedrooms upstairs and the bathroom, Me and James had the downstairs front room which contained a bed, a wardrobe and a table, that was it luckily we had a few bits to make it homely, Our other housemates was nice luckily we got along with them in room next to us there was a young guy around early 20s he was hilarious and soon learnt his name was Carl, Upstairs Mandy he was a funny character slightly strange but really friendly, he intrigued me he was different and proud of it too though the other housemates didn't like him much, Then there was Newton nicknamed so as he loved his beer and very rarely saw him about but he was a nice chap too mid-50s, then the last room upstairs above ours, that unfortunately we have had few run-ins with a strangely a family that live in room above us (yes a man, wife & their 1 yr. old baby in a shared house) there are Polish I think he is and lady is Maldivian, she doesn't much like me I understand that by names she calls me in her native tongue (oh gosh I'm thankful to Google translate) I was able to record and translate one day and I was an English (insert name for a female dog) I reported to police as hate crime and was me who got the tell off and told to leave them alone....hello cuntstable evidence?

◆ ◆ ◆

Life continues and we had many fun times together James and I, such as the night it snowed the first winter back in Doncaster, oh what fun we had, we lived near the Town fields which is one of Doncaster's biggest open spaces and a place me and James enjoyed walking in as was tree lined and so beautiful any time of day/year and so on this snowy day me & James decided at just after midnight to go for a walk in the snow to the Town fields as with living at the coast we hardly ever saw any snow and when we did it hardly settled because of the salt in the air from the sea it just thawed, it certainly did not ever get like this was now the snow was fluffy and huge white flakes we both started feeling a bit giddy and very much like kids! I should mention we had both had a little bit to drink by this time after all it was a Friday night and after a hour or so we started feeling a bit cold so we decided to head home but we thought it would be funny to each roll a huge snowball home up across the town fields and try to get them all the way home, It was around 3 streets to ours then we planned to place them upon each other to make a giant snowman decorate it then go to bed, we rolled them home with lots laughter, from us both and all clubbers that passed us going home as by this time it was going on for around 2 to 3am... Not long after we finally reached home and had 1 half snowballs left, The biggest one looked like a half-eaten cupcake... we plonked it in the front garden and went to bed the smaller one we just abandoned near front gate we was both so cold and tired by this point but that was the best fun I had encountered in many years, A few months later we was offered a flat upstairs above our landlords office, we jumped at the chance of once again having our own place, a home again with our own private toilet, we remained here still in the same village for a year or so but in this time my knee had dislocated, first time in a long time and this time it did not go right, I could not put any weight on it at all and Drs gave me crutches and referred me to Hospital to a rheumatologist, because of the flat being upstairs I struggled and in 2013 we got an offer of a council home of a ground floor flat as I had by now unfortunately suffered bad health deterioration and have since been diagnosed with joint hypermobility and fibromyalgia, I'm now classed as disabled from working and James is now my full-time career, we was given a 2 bedroom ground floor flat in the centre of Doncaster and I am pleased to say I've had contact with my children, was only once or twice but it is a start right, my mum met me in town and she brought along one of my kids, another time was a different kid but it wasn't enough or regular enough to build a relationship up with them!

Each time I saw them my mum was saying that the kids was acting up and misbehaving for her after seeing me and then saying they didn't wish to see me and how they was saying they still hated me etc. she then went on to say how she would never give up trying even if was last thing she did on her death bed she would get my kids talking to me again but I knew I couldn't trust my mum at this point sadly she had many times previously in my past and recently shown me as much and I suspected she was possibly lying and truth really was that the kids had not even said that at all and it was most possible it was only my mum saying it as she unfortunately is known for lying, I knew I had to try clear my name fully with the social services and fight to see my kids so I carried on my fight, never gave up, I sought an appointment with the director of children's services I was told that wasn't an option when I rang the social services department but I was not accepting that as a answer so I went into council offices refused to leave without an appointment with the Director of children's services and how no one lower would do, I obtained one within 20 minutes! How that is for achieving something I was earlier told was not possible to achieve...... I have since learnt anything is possible if you truly desire it enough and refuse to accept no or cant or wont as answers.

A few weeks later I had my appointment with Mr Bloggs the Director of children social services in Doncaster and he told me there was no reason at all I couldn't see my kids, I asked if had to be supervised and he said No not at all, If your mum needed a babysitter she could ask you and you could do it, it is up to your mum no one else!

Since 2009 to 2013 my mum & social services had kept kids from me telling me I could not see them and that my mum could do nothing though she wanted too and that I definitely could never see them unsupervised until they was 14... all of it my mum had said was again LIES, Mr Bloggs even went on to say it'd be my best interest to get on with my mum as she was my best chance of seeing my kids as if she asked me to babysit I could! I left totally shocked... An admittance id did nothing at all to warrant losing my kids as if had then 1 why wasn't I ever charged or even questions asked? 2 why he just say all that n say I can be left unattended with my kids... omg!

OLIVE BRANCH

Obviously, I took Mr Blogg's advice and slowly started texting my mum saying I had put the past to past as she had advised me and I wanted us to have a relationship and be close again if she wanted that too and deep down I guess I honestly do miss my mum, we did share many good times as I myself become a mum and together on holiday as adults we shared many good times, but that doesn't take the bad away and I hope we can build a relationship but I'm being cautious as this is mainly about my children and me seeing them too, well eventually she met me and we decided fresh start was best bet and we continued to try fix and build a relationship, we didn't meet often but occasionally my mum would meet me and have one of my kids with her which was more than I dared hope for only downside was that it was never planned nor ever structured which made it harder as I never knew if that was going be last time I saw them again... Or if not when will I see them again, I loved those days but they destroyed me too for a long time afterwards I would cry and be generally really low in my moods and then I'd see one of them again and the whole cycle repeated like this my physical and mental health failing me greatly... My relationship with James suffering, my family (nanna, aunt, cousins) all failing, friends are gone already... I am a mess... I need help, I realise this now, not that I've not tried to get the help enough times, I have been therapy and been to Drs they already had me on lots of tablets at this point for my ailments, it's a wonder I don't rattle. I know though I must do something so off back to Drs, this time I had 12 weeks of counselling which did help, she stated she feels I have PTSD and possibly bipolar too. I was advised to write all my emotions down and this is where I am right now, (apart from its now 2019 not 2014 like moment in book) so let us rewind back to 2014 which is currently where we are in my emotional rollercoaster ride of a timeline.

I've just finished counselling Talking therapy course which was 12 weeks long and I am feeling slightly stronger in myself mentally things now seem clearer yet I still feel I don't know who I am, I feel slightly lost and have million more questions than answers but I also know that what had happened to me in my past really was not my fault in any shape, way or form, the guilt I feel is normal but I shouldn't hold on to it as I should not feel it as I did nothing wrong to feel guilty about, the people who abused me did, that word abuse, the first time my therapist said that to me I burst into tears, I knew it was deep down but I'd denied it was abuse, all these years and I had without knowing locked all the bad memories away but the therapy and writing this unlocked some of them big style but there is still a lot I aint fully unlocked/recalled so much still patchy and unclear but I wouldn't at this point believe it that my mum was also guilty of neglecting me, I didn't want to believe it, apart from James my mum was the only other person I had in my life I was sooo confused, new questions going through my head but by end of the 12 weeks the therapist had really helped me and suggested a self-esteem course (which never did get the invite to attend), I had decided I wanted to improve my life and show my children I wasn't a waste of time nor energy and show them the correct attitude to have in life and also I wanted to prove it to myself that I was able and intelligent enough to have a qualification to my name I also wanted teach my kids that school, work etc. was important. I found an online course and I started studying and over the next few years I passed quite a few qualifications, I obtained a NVQ Level 2 in Business & Admin, NVQ level 2 in Sales

& Marketing and NVQ 2 in Equality & Diversity, I left school with no GCSE so this is huge to me, I proudly told my mum and she laughs and says oh how urm great (in a sarcastic voice) but your disabled so face it, you can't work, and you're in no fit state to do so nor will be and you need to accept that is your future... It's getting quite difficult to bite my tongue but least I'm hearing more about my kids, etc.

My mum has been ringing me often recently as she has been having major issues with well all of the children in one shape or form, This time it is Damien he is in my mum's own words 'still a nightmare' apparently he always has been badly behaved since he first started residing with my mum, she goes on to tell me that the things he is up to is things such as he steals money out her purse, lies about why he's late from school even if he's only 20 minutes late my mums on phone telling me saying how bad he is that he is late again and how she's had enough of him and my mum then goes on to ask me why he is doing it, I explain to her I do not see any of my kids often enough to have a relationship with them to know them well enough to tell you the answer to such a question mum I only wish I could be more helpful but apart from support you I can't so explain to me why do you think him late on bus is him lying, My mum then goes on to say that she knows for a fact at least 1 bus has gone past top of her lane and how he should have been on that bus as he normally is and how Damien will just use excuse of he's either lost his ticket or bus did not come, I said try just asking him please don't just loose it, but she didn't answer, Instead all I hear is 'Your mum is on the phone she knows what you are up to and I would not get mouthy if I was you' Damien responded but I honestly could not hear what he said as was almost a whimper rather than a confident spoken teenager, I felt so sad hearing him and so angry too I call to my mum on phone she answers but not before yelling at Damien to go to his room and stay there, she then said sorry about that but he is aggressive and hits out at her too so she has to get like that with him first and then she says about if he's not around them being centre of attention he's spending all his time alone in his bedroom alone refusing to speak to anyone, it breaks my heart the thought he is suffering like this, my uncle Edward tells me often that he's been to visit Garry his mate who lives down the lane from where my mum is now living which is in a Travelling community that Garry is owner of and my mum's landlord and Uncle Edward informed me how he had heard my mum or Hazel yelling at one of the kids often as he drove past the bottom of her gate, now her yard is a good 25+ foot long and that's just in direction of gate, so he really should not have heard her so how loud was they yelling especially as the door was also shut to the bungalow, or how he's popped in to my mums and seen one of my kids often Katie or Damien sat on the cold hard wooden kitchen floor facing the fridge freezer cross-legged arms folded sat silent for one reason or another, upon my uncle telling my daughter on this occasion to get up my mum instructed she remained there as she was there for a reason... My uncle felt disgusted but torn he didn't know what to do so he left and informed me, I hit roof upon hearing this, started looking into things more searching internet to learn the law on child and family court law, on mothers rights, on special guardianship orders, anything and everything I spent hours upon hours for months and months researching, learning my rights and in meantime grabbing any opportunity I could to spend time with my mum in hope of her fetching one of my kids along which sometimes happened oh how I lived for that few hours I got to see my kids I wished it was each of them I saw but it was always Dean with my mum and either Katie or Rory I do not know why, I asked my mum once why Damien was never with her ever and she replied he's too bad behaved, I can't take him anywhere and he says he doesn't want to go anywhere with me so what can I do, I had to accept it as didn't want to push her further and risk not seeing any of them, I had this hatred inside me when I looked at my mum at this time because I'd read court papers for first time since 2009 recently with a more clearer head and I now fully understood them and it wasn't confusing at all, the long words, the terms they use I had educated myself and learnt it all and all the historical court and social work papers indicated that my mum was the one in 2009 that had in the first instance, My own mum had been the one that had rang social services and reported me and made up most the terrible lies.... Thanks for that mum what makes you so perfect by the way how did you become qualified in maternal ways, caring and compassionate enough to pass judgement like that?

She had also told them that when she had collected them at the time when my car had broken down and I couldn't get back from Nottingham that my kids was black and blue and was dirty and covered in head lice! They certainly wasn't any of those things when I left them with Barry that Friday night, The report also stated my mum had reported how the kitchen cupboards was empty and house a mess when she had collected the kids and it didn't help that the neighbours were I used to live at time, who were also my mums friends and also she knew them from when we lived in Stainford as a kid and she somehow got them to make reports too saying they'd seen my kids on streets alone, what they failed to add on is the fact my children yes in end did play out in street after one of the parents knocking on my door asking if they could as they was stood outside and was happy to keep eye on them while they played with their children and they was stood watching them all the time and I often checked on them too and asked if they was still ok etc. but no that wasn't on report, I was gob smacked at how I hadn't seen nor realised any of this back in 2009 It was only recently I truly understood all these legal forms, it shows how badly my mental health was affected during the court case and social work ordeal in 2009 I answered questions I was asked by social services, I had a mental capability assessment that indicated I had issues and demonstrated basic parenting skills as Dr Pants a phycologist had said that my lack of skills as a parent and my mental state was a direct result of my own upbringing, Another report on my mum by a Dr on a medical report stated that my mums health was not good enough to raise 4 young children and she'd likely suffer doing so, I am still trying to obtain answers today to this question which is given this information why was my children placed into my mums care and her given a special guardianship order?

I continued my fight and I decided armed with my new knowledge in law and knowing more about my right's and knowing my children was in great danger from what I had experienced as a child and was still suffering now plus the fact I and my husband had witnessed recently a quite bad incident where one week day my mum had picked me and James up and while driving down the road in her 7 seater mobility car, Katie in front passenger seat as she was off school ill this day had headache and belly ache bless her but my mum brought her to cash and carry to cheer her up, me and James in the backseat and on way back home Katie asked my mum to bash her Terrys chocolate orange as it was too hard for her to crack it open herself and she couldn't open it, my mum grabbed it from Katie while driving turned to Katie and hit her on the head quite loudly and laughed her head off said there you go Katie done, I said mum what the actual F.... Why would you do that...seriously that could have really done damage? Katie are you ok? Katie said urm yes, it hurts a bit but I am ok thank you, my mum was still laughing and said oh come on it was not that hard I'm only having fun, I was horrified and looked at James who looked like he was going to explode or be sick I couldn't tell but he wasn't amused nor was I, My mum dropped me home and I spoke to James about this and this is when James for first time opened up and said he always knew was something about my mum but he didn't know what but now he sees she's a neglectful, spiteful evil person and those kids should not be with her she's clearly got some sort of personality disorder and those kids was at risk big style, I asked James If I got my kids back would he support me, He obviously said of course I will always.

In 2014 I applied to court for access to my children to hopefully gain visitation rights and during the case I obtained many more court papers and reports as I represented myself throughout the case it meant I got all the paperwork that my mums solicitor also had access too, I learnt this would assist me greatly rather than trust in someone who only cared about pound signs rather than justice being done and I wrote an in depth letter accompanying the application to court explaining all my concerns has I knew the Law system would quite possibly see me as a worthless human being who had even though was many a years ago had her kids removed and was no way getting them back and that no matter what I said they'd not believe me and quite wrong or rightfully judge me by a past rather than what they see in front them now as I had not yet had any luck with the social services in clearing my name I keep hitting a brick wall so the fight for that is still ongoing separately from this court case and since they'd already judged me many years ago and in the laws eye's people do not change and they obviously had access to my past records I knew how they'd view me from the start instead of re-evaluating me as I stand before them today, so I knew I had my work cut out ahead of me. I have had people make me feel worthless and bad, feel guilty and shame when I have no reason to feel this way, I made mistakes, we all do in one way or form but through all my pain over years I have met a lot of wonderful people and not so wonderful and I have witnessed the not so wonderful become such kind, caring and this in fact shown me many times people DO change and I certainly had in many ways for starters I have matured, I am more confident in myself (though I admit their still work to be done in this area yet) most of all I now had control of my own mind and life and was starting to develop my personality and was I know this sounds crazy but discovering who I am as a person too, I made sure along with my court application I also attached a letter of statement along with photocopies of family photographs of me and my kids on days out or family holidays etc. and other valuable evidence which proved useless in the end it appeared to be largely ignored, even though the reports from school the courts had obtained and I have copies of from certain organisations was saying Damien had bruises on him amongst other worrying reports which showed multiple times the children's social services had been involved and investigated the various multiple reports involving my mum and kids since my children had been placed with her they had only been with her for 5 years and on these new court reports it claims there was more than 5 incidents reported within that time, so that's more than 1 report a year why was this not being took seriously? My kids, my kids schools etc. had made complaints against my mum whilst in her care, yet they choose to believe my mum over my evidence or even their own facts as when I questioned why there was 5 reports yet each one was never took seriously quite clearly with my children still residing their at risk they informed me that if any of the previous reports I had mentioned was ever proven to have been right the kids would not still be saying they wanted to remain living with her like they are saying plus the children presented clean, well looked after and happy around nanna so they had no concerns, I went on to explain about how I felt as a child growing up which was hard to do and how I was and am still suffering and can't lose my mum even though she hurts me, it's what happens to abused people It does not mean the abuse does not happen or hasn't happened in fact it means it has happened over a long period and mentally and physically the person is beaten and feels like they can't physically live or cope without their abuser in this instant my mum I know this as it's how I felt.

I poured my heart out to that judge yet regardless of the school reports that also stated Damien and Katie suffered unexplained behavioural issues & bruises, was often late for school and there education was suffering, homework often not done and such like the judge just did not see this at all, I do not understand why but yet again their reaction was that there was no evidence found upon investigation that Jossalynn and Hazel had family intervention for a short period of time I enquired into what family intervention was and I was told the role of the Family Worker (Early Intervention) is to provide a mixture of individual and group interventions with parents, carers, children and young people with additional needs up to the thresholds for social care involvement to improve outcomes for children, so clearly they agreed they was indeed issues within the home but that after the early intervention the family appeared to need no further help so they closed the case, (It is a shame they did not investigate my case they'd have realised the truth or even have offered me this service to help me instead of just acting abruptly and rashly without facts and evidence)

The way I saw it right now after this was the judge appeared to see nothing more than this old disabled lady who took in her grandkids this angel of society surely can't be at fault right....
.....

An organisation that works with children during court cases also went to see the children during this court case and was asked how they felt, if they was happy etc. and if they wished to see me, again my children stated they didn't wish to see me or receive any form of contact with me. All my concerns I'd mention where just ignored, you see I was going through all this not solely for my needs as I would always and was now only acting in my kids best interests, whether they are with me or in a care home or another family member I knew any of those options was better than with my mum and I had heard enough horror stories about care homes over the years too so I really didn't want that option for my babies, I just wanted my children safe I didn't want my kids growing up being like me having mental health issues, friendships affected, whole life affected and I knew by being raised in the same environment I encountered I didn't wish how I was at moment and how I had been with my health what with my mental health and how my lack of parental care as a child had directly resulted me as an adult in many ways, shape and forms how I am/act or have acted in past has showed me that much, I even now still have lots of healing to do before I can say it's all in my past, It's difficult and I have missed out on much joys of life and seriously would do anything to make sure my children did not have that future, everyone has the right to a life that is threes, freedom and right's to make their own choices in life right or wrong it is how we progress and learn in life.

In the end the courts ruled that I had only indirect contact in means of birthday and Christmas cards and only had contact if children wished to see me, the positive side is I had got the courts to at least add on to the original Guardianship some new orders that instructed I was to have a photograph of each of my children at least a few times a year from my mum and a school photograph once a year and I would get school reports sent to me which was at least something but sadly I still felt the court system and judge just viewed me as well I'd say scum but no that's probably bit harsh but they definitely saw me as a grieving mother that wanted her babies and was saying anything to get them back, I so wish that was case but it truly isn't.

I knew my children were not safe, they might be fed, have toys and rules but they are not having a child's life at all they was not hanging out with their mates after school, never went to any hobbies or anything, there life was simply just home and Katie & Rory and if he wished to Dean also was taken to the Livery Yard each evening after school to poo pick & other livery duties as and when instructed to do so, very little or no horse riding as there was never time, by time the yard duties was done it was going on for tea time so it was then back home for their teas then they had a bath followed by homework if they had time to do any then supper and bed at 7pm. That was my eldest 2 lives with my mum from ages of Katie aged 8yrs, Rory aged roughly 9yrs until well there adults now and only recently stopped this, every day Mon to Fri and all day Sat and Sunday Katie and Rory was told by Jossalynn that this was an expected duty of them to learn responsibility and after her taking them in when no one else would it was least they could do especially as she had bought them each the pony and told they had a duty for its care and should also put their pocket money toward it's care too or she would get rid of them if they had any more issues with helping out, Now I agree with my mum if they'd asked for a horse then yes it was their responsibility to care for their horses but they'd not asked it was bought to basically 'buy' my kids to say they wanted remain with Jossalynn rather than go home where they'd have no horses etc. but I felt they needed to mix with other children outside school hours too and have chance to just be kids and have fun do kid things too which they never did, they didn't even have simple things in their bedrooms such as a TV, none of the kids had a console or a phone, only Dean had these items, the younger three was not allowed to touch each other belongings my mum made it clear they was only ever to use their own items.

As for Damien he never went out, he never did anything with my mum, always left at home with Hazel whom also never left her home, Hazel spent all her time cleaning, cooking and doing the household chores basically she was like a slave for my mum as my mum did not do housework claiming that Hazel was her carer and it was her duty to do it, now this may be ok if Hazel was in good health but she wasn't she was getting quite old by now still a big lady, she had epilepsy and could barely walk more shuffled her feet and slides places, often she has fallen and badly hurt herself, she's in desperate need of care herself never mind caring for everyone in the home, even though I should hate Hazel given my past neglect and how she's treated me but I can't hate her after seeing her like this before the court case on one of rare times my mum had invited me to her home and I witnessed Hazels poor health, I could not feel angry, I actually feel sorry for her and wished she too would see that she too is being abused and being treat like a slave, my mum has in past told me that she has Hazels bank card in her own purse were it stays put and how Jossalynn withdraws Hazels money and keeps it each week, I didn't believe her and told my mum as much so she showed me the bank card, she had 4 bank cards in her purse all Barclays bank I'm guessing not all my mums but obviously I do not know for sure it could be legit, miracles do happen right?

Me and my mum did not speak for a while after the court case, but a few months later my mum texted me asking me to ring her, I did so and she mentioned how the court had cost her such huge solicitor fees in excess of three thousand pounds, I said why did you just not represent yourself as I did, she said because I was scared, I laughed, she laughed and she said how about a fresh start, stupidly I agreed and life continued.

Once around this time which is now early 2015 my mum and Hazel had argued and my mum rang me she was laughing so hard I could hardly understand her I aid ok what's so funny and she went on to say what she'd done something funny to Hazel I said dare I ask? She replied I fed her Angel Cake and Gravy for tea and Hazel ate it and enjoyed it I laughed n said yeah right you possibly did feed her it yes but bet she never ate it, Hazel then came on the phone and laughed and said I did eat it and it was nice I replied and said ok your very strange human being..... my mum was still living in a bungalow type thing on the travellers community within the Doncaster region and had 1 horse on her land and a 3 doored single stalled stable being built, there was also a 14ft touring caravan that they claim Mari lives in for benefit purposes but she does not do so at all for starters she can't even walk up n down the 3 small caravan steps without falling backwards, she does so badly require personal care really herself. There are also other caravan's electric static further up the lane in another area belonging to the same landlord and another house in front of my mums which at this time is only partial built. It really is much rather like a construction site type place and has been like this for the last well 8 years since I remember from when my uncle lived on site well before my mum moved on so quite possibly longer, not at all what I would say is a great environment for raising kids of any age, In fact truth be told I would not live their if was just myself and James it to me was that poor state of repair, but for some again very strange and unknown to me reasoning beyond my abilities to think the social workers have stated it's a perfect home environment, It's rare that my mum invites me up to hers and previously I had only got to see the living room so today I took full advantage to look around at the place my mum called home and I wish I hadn't as now I was more worried about were my children was residing as really was and I am sorry if you reading this Garry but my mum's place really was/is in such bad state of repair for rent being charged the kitchen floor was not even in a good state, I'll try and explain the layout and issues in the home I saw as I quickly glanced around the place when my mum was showing me around, You enter my mum's home a chalet type property one story in height, sort of a dirty white colour, there is 2 steps up to the front door which leads directly into the living room that has a huge stone pillar in the middle that is one of the main supporting beams for the whole property but why in middle of the living room? To the right is rest of living room which does not look too bad in state of repair and décor the cream sofa is well very black in places but that can be excused right , to left is a step down into the kitchen which I am shocked to see contains a single worktop, a cooker, a washer, fridge and a chest freezer and a sink all in very bad state and the floor was laminate and poorly laid and near the sink it was up in places, easy to trip up on for sure, Then a small dark dingy passage that the bedrooms led off, first bedroom on left is Deans room I didn't see in that he did not wish us to go in, Then my mums room with 2 single beds in and a number of gym equipment again looked ok, then Damien and Rory's room simple really a bed each, wardrobe each, chest draws to share and couple of books and a small plastic box my mum informs me they have one each which all their private belongings are in, I enquire where Katie sleeps to which my mum replied the touring caravan I said the one benefit office thinks Hazel rents from Garry? I got no reply just a 'look' I knew meant shut up, the bathroom is possibly the worst room, the toilet inside is black with stains looked like it had not been cleaned in a long time, outside isn't much better either the white parts were pretty dark brown in places, the toilet seat looked pretty stained in places too I honestly had seen public toilets in cleaner states, the sink was dirty as was the shower that was caked in lime scale, the window had thick mould on it as did most the bathroom area.

It Its summer 2015, me and my mum have tried moving on from the past and having a relationship for the sake of the kids, putting past to past, it's hard but hey I'm at my kids home, yes they are currently at school but it's 2 pm she's not asked me leave yet... Might I see them?

Well, that was a very interesting visit indeed, I was sat on my mum's well was supposed be white but was now a nice mix of brown and black with bits of cream furry leather sofa when in walked Katie & Damien, Katie smiles but that's it and says she's going to her room and Damien looks catches my eye and has a certain look I can't describe, I would not know how to then he turns and goes in to his bedroom without saying a single word to anyone... but I saw it... I knew that look, he does want to see me. That's all I needed to know not to ever give up, I had a new fight all of me now...

SHOCKING DISCOVERY

Well it's now the start of march 2016, last few months have been crazy ride of an emotional ride with my mum and I one moment we ok, the next she's turned all funny and acting strange and now last few month's my nan took very ill and she was in out Drs so much with various complaints that we was all so very worried about her, the whole family seemed to be pulling together right now which never happened we was all that worried, then she ended up being rushed to the A&E at our local hospital my mum had collected her and after checking her out the Dr actually wanted to send her home, my mum and my nan normally do not get on at all but my nan was that ill she had asked for my mum to take her A&E in her car rather than wait for an ambulance and that's why my mum was there at hospital right now, If my mum had not been at hospital and my nan had gone home as Drs insisted my nanna maybe not be with us today, you see after they finally agreed to admit my nanna and do further tests over the following few days it turned out my nan had a little cyst type thing behind her heart that needed open-heart surgery to remove it because of its location or something but my nanna needed transferring to Sheffield hospital in the City for the operation which happened not long afterwards, the surgery went well thank heavens and my nan made an amazingly quick recovery for her age I mean she was 75 years old that very next month not that you would know it to look at my nanna, well before she got ill anyhow she still looked no older than 65 and acted like she was too, but since being in hospital and being ill she had lost lots of weight and looked so frail but

she still fought on and was soon back home & pretty much almost fully back on her feet by middle April, but during my nans recovery one day my uncle whilst we was visiting my nanna after her recovery in Sheffield hospital took me, James & Chucky to this family day room, sat us down and directly and bluntly stated he was dying, Chucky laughed and rolled her eyes as if she was thinking omg here we go again as I am first to admit my Uncle did like to have something wrong with him he loved attention but no not this time I saw something in his eye a sadness then he swallowed/gulped...OMG reality suddenly hit me ..
...I realised he meant it, my precious Uncle was dying, no, no can't, don't... I ran from the room... I think anyhow as I honestly don't recall it clearly, but next thing I do recall was me stood in the hospital hallway outside the room and my uncle looking at me, holding me, telling me it was ok and to breathe and calm down and listen to him and that he was ok with it and he didn't want sadness, that he wasn't scared and that he was telling me as he needed to and wanted me to know, I was horrified, sadness engulfed me and there he for first time ever that he loved me very much then went on to say how James was the man for me and I wasn't to let him go and we should marry as I'd not find anyone better!

Over those next few weeks life pretty much carried on as before, no one really gave anything else much thought, I was taking my nanna out places growing very close to her indeed and this caused bit of jealousy within the family strangely chucky started acted weirdly, like I couldn't go anywhere with nanna or she would ring multiple times asking what time she would be home or asking if she was ok, If I visited my nanna she would be their each time, James used to go visit my nanna with me often but Chuckys behaviour was growing more and more strange, she was now bending over in front of James with low cut tops on and almost showing everything she had on top half or she would make a remark about him, this made James feel very uncomfortable and he stopped visiting as even nanna had spotted and told Chucky to stop she had a serious relationship too, it was all very strange behaviour indeed and I also stopped going as much, My mum was also acting weird again with me, she had hardly bothered to contact me and she nor I hardly saw rest of family still at this time, and life just carried on like this for few months really that is until that day I'll never forget.

Me & James had just filled up our car with petrol at one of our local supermarket petrol stations and was it was a scorching hot dry humid day for so early in the year was only May, I had a vest top on and felt a squirt of water on my back as I was filling up my car and I thought what the......little monkies, Ok which car contained the kid that had just squirted me with the water pistol? I spun around ....No cars on the forecourt nor anyone around either and the petrol pump was under a roofed shelter and definitely was not raining anyhow.... How strange, I finished filling up and paid by card at pump and as I got in my car my phone starts to ring, My mum...well my mums number but my son Dean my eldest on phone quite panic-stricken and calling me mum (something definitely isn't right he never calls me mum its always Emma!) I ask him what's wrong, he tells me it's my uncle Edward they are switching life support off and I should get there quickly! WHAT!!!!!

I wasn't even aware he was in hospital in first place (I later found out that he was in their 3 days before I got that call) no one thought to tell me at the time he was rushed in like but all of the rest family knew and they had all been at the hospital visiting over last few days, what must they all think of me not visiting when the fact was I wasn't even made aware my one and only uncle who I loved dearly was in hospital, like I did not matter to them or I did not even pass their minds to inform me when they was informing rest of family......thanks family I feel so loved.

I obviously flew to that hospital which was luckily only 3 minutes away from the location I was at but it felt like an hour especially trying to find somewhere to park! I reached my uncles bedside and I knew as soon as I saw him....even though machines said he was alive that the man laid there was not my uncle, It was sadly clear to me that he'd already gone, only way I can describe it is he looked empty his lovely kind caring face contained this empty vacant look, his baby blue eyes that was always full of expression they now just was just staring upwards and also empty and dull, I didn't know what to say/do so I just kissed my uncles cheek told him I loved him dearly and I just went and sat with everyone else in the family room and said nothing unless I was spoken too!

That same day only a few hours later on 12th May 2016 sadly my uncles Life support machine was switched off he was 56 years old, He died of multi-organ failure the brain scan revealed he had less than 1% of brain activity, We all said our goodbyes beforehand some choose to be there during the machine being switched off, I could not do so, My mum swears I was there but I'm sure I wasn't, I was asked afterwards if I wanted go in say goodbye but I said no, I couldn't bare seeing him like that again, I gave everyone a cuddle and I went home in a state of shock.

Those following few days was a total blur, his funeral hit my nanna & us all very hard, me and my mum met up at the catholic church none our family is catholic but my uncle and my mum got baptised when they joined the catholic choir and church as teenagers, my uncle had a beautiful white horse drawn carriage for his funeral which was leaving from a 2 minute walk up the road from my uncles brother in-laws house, His daughters and a lot of family and friends took behind the carriage and walked in procession behind my uncle to the church which was so lovely and touching, Me and my mum stayed together throughout the ceremony sat on the front row I felt awkward as my nanna was sat behind me and I knew she should have been sat there but she insisted I sat with my mum as she wanted to sit with her youngest daughter Mary and her two daughters Candy and Chucky but it was a horrible atmosphere it really was obvious everyone there hated each other, It was beautiful and quite shameful how people was acting at a funeral all at same time but very typical of my family too!

At the wake I sat with my nanna, it was horrible the division in the family even at times like this they can't be mature and unite for the sake of a loving memory shared of a lost soul took too soon, It's a disgrace, makes me ashamed to call them my family and making it so obvious too there was my mum and another member of the Ward side of family the Leggs side do not get on with at all sat a few tables away from me, James and my nanna along with us was Candy, Mary and few others then across room was some others I didn't know and then at other side was another group people also at another pub in the village there was also another wake held for my uncle organised by his wife and her side of the family it really was ridiculous, It's obvious everyone feels so uncomfortable, I make my excuses and leave I need to get out of this situation, it's too much!

Life continues pretty much as close to normal and dare I say nice for a year or two, I was spending time with my nanna again I was taking her out places to try help her get over her grief and take her away from it all and we built up a very close relationship and visited some lovely places together, My Auntie Mary Leggs my mums youngest sister and her two daughters, my three kids, my younger cousins (Mary's children) Chucky Seaman and Candy Seaman and Franky Banks, Candies Daughter Winter and Chuckie's son Ryan was all seeing each other often and built up a close or as I thought loving relationship and I often took them out places as by now I had a car and as I was the only one in my family to have a car so was often the family taxi,

I didn't mind though I was just happy to have them in my life, to finally have a family around me and feel happy, This didn't last though, you see Chucky was used to doing everything with our nanna and spending a lot of time with her being her youngest grandchild she was used to being babied in the family and she really wasn't amused at amount time our nanna was spending with me and she started showing me as much, one day she rang me demanding to know why I had upset our nanna, I was totally confused and said what on earth are you on about I was not long off the phone to nanna and we was chatting and laughing as usual, nanna certainly was not crying when I hung up, but chucky was having none of it, I rang my nanna and asked her and she said I don't know she's got it in her head you have upset me but I have told her you aint just ignore her so I said I would do but a few hours after the call I got a notification saying Candy had written on my wall on Facebook wall, this was so unlike her so I logged straight on and read and then reread what she had put it took me 10 minutes to finally realise yes she had put what I thought publically for ALL to see, she had only gone and written that I was a paedophile along with a whole book of abuse! I was gobsmacked and horrified and immediately panicked about how many could've seen those vile lies and maybe believed them, people get stabbed etc. for this type stuff true or not rumours can have fatal consequences as we all unfortunately see in the news quite often, I was scared, angry and upset, I rang candy she started yelling threatening me, saying my mum had told them years ago and I made them sick so I asked her if that was case why did she let me near her own daughter huh cause she knows it is lies she went on to say so why did your mum say it then huh...why did you lose your kids if not that, I said I'll show you court papers I have nothing to hide hunni and she slammed phone down after saying they'd be through alright but not to read anything, so that is why my kids didn't want to see me omg my mum was telling people this, now I see why the people in Stanford in 2009 threatened to petrol bomb my home with me in it.... at the time the threats made no sense but now, omg this is real, my own mum.... No way surely not, why would she say such things?

I hung up, messaged candy and demanded she told me more, she went on abusing me saying it explains why social services took my kids, how they believed my mum and how I was a liar, I simply told her I'd go police, I set the status to me only in privacy settings and I screenshot them and contacted the police, at first they did not wish to help me tried saying no crime had took place, I insisted because it was public for over 4,000 people to see it was indeed a huge issue and needed sorting asap and they held a duty to protect me and I insisted they did so, they agreed to go speak to Candy and went to her work as she would not answer her front door, that was it, my whole family turned on me even though the police had informed Candy I held no record at all and I had not even ever been investigated nor arrested in my life for anything and was in fact the role citizen they still turned on me...... for ringing police to clear my name...... I know family do not ring police on family EVER but come on sometimes there really is no option and this wasn't to press charges it was to simply clear my name! Nope the family would not see it this way and they all stopped speaking to me.

It's now December 2019 just 1 week from Xmas and am facing my 3rd Christmas without my family in my life, not that we ever was invited anywhere on Christmas Holiday period anyhow, it has always just been me and James on Xmas day, we do not know what it is to celebrate with loved ones and be part of a family, we only have each other but least we are happy, but going back to time it is in book which is now roughly 2017 and It's now just me and James that is it, my mums not talking right and I'm no longer seeing kids at all, My mum only really rings me when she wants to moan at me about how one of my kids are misbehaving, or if they've done something amazing or if my mum and one of kids has done something together she'll ring me, tell me, I loved and hated these moments, I loved them as I got to hear about my babies life's, what their up to and I got to ask questions without her biting my head off but I hated them too as I felt jealous and wished it was me doing these things with my kids, it should be me, but I always was careful, bit my tongue and kept quiet, I let the tears flow after the call, I wrote down how the calls went to get my feelings out, I started writing and before long I had wrote a journal of my life, a diary which gave me idea of writing it as a book, my life story so my kids could understand why I wasn't the best mum, why my head wasn't as it really should have been while they was in my care, by writing a book I would be able to show them that I did care, that they were always and still are very much loved and that I would give my life so they could live, That is what being a parent is all about, I made mistakes but I wasn't given the chance to put my mistakes right and that was wrong on every level, Surely the only way to improve society and improve as a species and develop within ourselves is to make mistakes, learn from them not repeat them and improve..... But if not given that chance how can one do so?

How do you tell someone all of this I have so far written in words in 1 sentence when you know all you might get chance to say if I saw my kids in street is a quick 20 second sentence before they told me to go away in not as nice words, you see my mum has turned them against me that much, she says she hasn't but what other reasoning is their? I also realised I wasn't alone, that many other people had also suffered as I have in one way, shape or form let it be sexual abuse, rape, mental torture, grooming, abuse, neglect all in childhood! All in UK, I seriously thought I was a rare occurrence but I realised around this time this certainly wasn't the case, I also learnt the Government our own country had brain washed us all to believe social services do not remove children for nothing, but sad truth is they do, and have, unfortunately mishandling and misbelieving evidence and not checking facts, etc. mistakes do happen, it should not happen but sadly it does, so does the abuse behind closed doors and this I realised needs to be also brought to the public's attention, so I relooked at my writing and realised I could with hard work turn this journal my therapist had me start and I'd written lots in maybe with lots hard work turn it into a fiction book based on real life events and hopefully help lots of people realise they too are not alone and that the help is out there and the support, love, kindness and happiness is there and I for one most certainly will be if you have no one else and to hopefully support and if it only helps just the one person then all the pain and suffering I had felt would not have been for nothing and that alone made me do this and so this is how the book and my story came about and is currently the point I am starting the book though that to you readers I know will be confusing so I'll explain before this chapter was my memories, they was all the things I could recall or have recalled yet I know there are huge gaps I still have blocked, pain I'm still suffering and flash backs and night terrors I suffer daily but I am happier, I am in a loving long term relationship common law married and anything written after this is written in the present as it is currently happening or happened, I plan on writing a little of this each few month's as I still yet do not think the ending is right after all I'm not seeing my kids and do not have answers yet.....

MY MUM MEETS TEEN YEARS!

O h my! It's 2017 well to be precise it is almost 2018 and boy has my mum had it bad these last months but you know what I am not being nasty but she did sort of ask for it all right? After all us, parents ask for it when we want a cute little baby without thought of these teenage years will fetch us but we have a duty once our child is born to protect, raise and care for it to best of our ability no matter what and my mum asked for it the moment she lied about me and reported me which led to my kids being removed from my care so she could get benefits and boost her ego by creating this fake life style she's created for herself were she's important and better than anyone else cause she has horses and socialises in the equestrian lifestyle of dressage and participating and watching horse shows etc. and if that sounds harsh it is because it's how I have had to become to survive what I have been through but it does not mean I care any less but in my mind the reasoning behind why she deserves it is really simple, she chose to lie about me because I had choose to move out of the town she lived she didn't like me making a choice for myself without even consulting her and she choose to take in my kids if she hadn't the social services said themselves I stood more chance of them being returned to me, why I do not know maybe cause there just isn't enough care homes plus keeping them altogether would have been difficult to do in care system so they'd have returned them to my care and investigated properly and my mum stood by and not just allow what had happened to me but participated in it too and was likely to allow it to most likely happen again at least mentally to my own children but I knew everyone who met my mum saw nothing more than an old lady that was in very poor state of health and yet saved her grandkids from a neglectful home and how she was sooo sweet and loving to do so and deserved some sort of medal..... All I can say and it still does hurt me to write and say or think such things as I still love my mum, she gave birth to me and gave me life, but I find it hard to think anything more than Oh yes what a fab lady my mum is, if only you knew the truth.... what an amazing little old disabled narcissistic lady is what you would really be saying when truth is my mum just needs help but until she accepts she too has past historical issues she is not facing she won't change and that is such a shame!

Sorry getting back on track ha-ha!

The kids each of them have been giving her nothing but complete misery for quite a while now for instance take our Dean from the age of well I would say a toddler he was a handful to be honest, for some reason as soon as he was potty trained he refused to wear undies, I'd go to my mums to see Dean and my mum and there my son Dean would be toddling around the flat in his birthday suit and nothing else this continued until he was around 9 years or so old, as a toddler Dean also had started hitting out at people if he couldn't get what he wanted Hazel suffered badly she often had a black eye from were Dean had thumped her or threw something and when I asked my mum why she let him she laughed and said it is funny when he does it, he is soo tiny, I mentioned to my mum about how he may have a few behavioural issues possibly adhd or something like that and maybe should mention it to her Drs, she told me he was fine and I was over reacting and stop being daft, Dean was quite spoilt growing up, my mum bought him anything he wanted he got right away and aged around 10 ish when his other siblings moved in he went completely off the rails, used to getting everything he wanted let it be latest console or gaming pc or designer clothing or even his food cooked but only food he asks for nothing else and getting all the attention and now suddenly this was gone as my mum could not no longer afford this with now having 4 children to provide for equally and he had to share my mums attention and Hazel no longer could respond straight away to his every whim as he was used too! Dean didn't want to share, he didn't know how to do so and this resulted in him starting to be very angry in his behavioural ways and attitude, This showed not just at his home with my mum, with everyone but also at school, he ended up in a behavioural unit, a school for kids with quite bad behavioural issues and can't cope in mainstream schools etc. He even managed to get kicked out of that too somehow and thought it was hilarious as did my mum! No school and no unit nowhere would take him, he was out of control and my youngest kids lived in this chaos! Dean now is 19 years old and is a stunning young man look wise with his olive tanned skin, brown eyes and dark hair he has a Greek type look to him and a cheek personality to match too but he has been diagnosed with psychosis so finds life quite difficult and often has rages (see mum I was right all those years ago if only you had listened to me) Dean is on benefits unable to work and lives at home with my mum still.

I tried telling social services, schools, and courts you name it but nope somehow my mum convinced them all was great I was just being malicious...HOW she does it? More to point how do these professionals not see it? It baffles me.

As for Katie she is now 17 just turned, looks the double of me so that's 3 of us looking like clones of each other with her blonde hair and blue eyes and high cheek bones she truly is beautiful, My daughter is very bossy and holds a quite fierce attitude she was clearly suffering too as my mum reports that by the age of 13 Katie was giving my mum lip, staying out late getting drunk with her mates, smoking and my mum suspected not just tobacco with her eyes and behaviour, generally acting up, I guess she was rebelling at being tightly controlled, never allowed out after school, no phone, no laptop, no access to internet at all really apart from at school.......again I raised my concerns, I rang social services and once again reported my concerns on how I could see my mum's treatment being impressed upon them and reflecting in their behaviours again I was ignored...WHY? This is getting too frustrating, what is it going to take before the authorities realise I am trying to save my children from depression and feeling mixed up as adults?

This fetches us to my youngest Damien he is 14 now and again is my clone literally I didn't realise boys could be double of their mums but WOW he has my high cheek bones, my jaw line, my everything look wise he was even super skinny and looked underweight like me, I never heard anything about him at all, none of the family reported ever seeing him like they did with others they would contact me and say seen whomever they are fine but whenever I asked after Reece the whole of my family stated they didn't know how he was as they the same as me have not seen him in years, It was like he didn't exist within the family, his name was never spoken and to me it felt a really horrible situation and I thought often about his future away from my mum as an adult and how he'd be alone and have no family nothing to fall back on just like I haven't any family I can call upon never mind his mental health will be affected and his job, love life possibly and I couldn't risk that, this causes me great stress and unnecessary worry but it is one I can't shift or shake off, I have tried, It was sooo strange that not one person had seen him though even my Uncle Edward said when he had visited my mum's he hardly saw or heard him, I used to go near kids schools to catch glimpse of him to make sure he was ok, It was the only way to get any peace of mind as I was so worried about him, They are my kids, yet me sitting in my car parked up the road from the bus stop they caught bus home, me sat in my car hiding watching Katie and Damien this felt sooo wrong, but those

2 minutes watching my kids play, it might be daft, but watching them be kids... Magical just knowing they was ok was a huge peace of mind and I did this weekly! People have asked why didn't I approach my children, answer is simple I didn't wish to upset my children just make sure they was ok!

Rory, he was just Rory bless him he never really put up a fuss as a kid ever even as a baby, Rory was getting on with life fantastically he was excelling in all he put his mind too and doing great in his special needs school, in fact doing amazing, winning lots of trophies and doing duke of Edinburgh gold award. He is showing signs of behavioural issues but as of yet these are mild but he does have Global Development Delay which is all round learning issues so I am extremely proud of everything he achieves not bad for someone drs said would not survive first night of his life! Well Done Rory!

My mum well what can I say about her and how she is right now..... She is 56 years old and has greying hair, most her teeth are rotten or missing altogether (she won't go dentist as has a deep fear of them) she only ever will be seen dressed in equestrian wear and her favourite perfume Eau De Horse or deodorant she must use is I believe called La Farm the smell of mucking out and not bathing..... honestly I just wish I could take my mum for a meal or shopping just once and she would smell nice, be clean and wear something not dirty or equestrian or at very least wash her hands as I recall taking my mum to Owston A very nice restraint in our area and for once she had worn jeans and a shirt and looked nice, we sat down at table, she reached for the menu and I noticed her finger nails... OMG... Yuk! I suddenly didn't feel so hungry, I aint exaggerating her hands were clean but her finger nails they was a different story, all around the edges and under the nail tip was dirt deep inside them, I looked closer I just said mother give me your hand and she did so but looked confused, I looked and sure enough you know your skin has little lines in it, well those lines was more defined by the dirt embedded into my mums fingers... I said omg mum look at your hands there dirty she said I know everyone's at yards go like that it's called hard work! I was shocked to say least and said not if you use soap, I was called a cheeky cow and she changed subject. I love my mum but clean isn't a word I would use to describe her at all unfortunately.

It's beginning of 2018 now and I've just had a call from my mum claiming Damien has stabbed her, she's had the police go there and she's ok it's only her hand she reassures me and that it was a few days ago now (so why she only just now telling me this?) she goes on to explain how he had slashed her hand by how my mum describes it Damien was yelling at my mum, being aggressive in his tone and body language so she was mouthing back at him, he grabbed a knife off the kitchen counter close to where they was arguing and came at my mum when she was laid down on sofa in living room and she held out her hand and grabbed the knife off him which caused my mum to cut her hand slightly as she grabbed the blade but it wasn't deep and the police had come out not long after the incident and that Damien had got arrested and was questioned at the station and few hours the same day he was released on bail but he was given a caution with a list of things he had to follow or be arrested again which made no sense to me but I said nothing and thought a lot I'd by now learnt this was the best way, she then went on to say he had written a letter after he'd stabbed her she had sent him to his room until the police arrived he then apparently had written a letter which my mum claims within the letter Damien admitted stabbing his nanna and saying he wish she had died and how he hated her and he would do it again etc., she said she'd show me it but never did ever show me it and that he was in serious trouble, none it makes any sense at all and to be honest the story is far too jumbled as for starters in 1 breath my mum stated she was laid on the sofa when Damien came at her in Livingroom and in next breath she informed me she was in kitchen stood up, so I honestly do not know which it was as when I enquired my mum told me she didn't say she was laid down where the hell did I get that from? Urmmm your mouth I reply to which she said you're getting worse love…. I don't bother going on I know it's pointless and say ok so go on mum carry on… I ask her again did you say Damien stabbed you for real I'm struggling to take all this in, I'm horrified. My mum then replies in a sad tone…'Yes love I am sorry I know he is your son but he stabbed me on my hand, it's ok to love', she goes on to say… 'He now has to see a youth offender worker until he's 18 called Emma', he has something called a community service order? Apparently, my mum has been told if Damien does any more bad behaviour he will be taken to court and he'll be removed from my mums care, she suddenly says she has to go and that's that, I come off phone and tell James everything, I am obviously worried sick and in tears, I know my son wishes to go into the Army this will mess that up for sure and again I am thrust straight back into my past feelings, In my head I am suddenly that young girl, feeling those dark painful feelings, thoughts…It's too much hearing it all again, I snap out of it as James holds me tight and soothes me and I tell James my worries what if Damien is acting out to escape the abuse I went through, what if he and the others are affected like I am as adults too, what if how they are being affected stops them from having friends, relationships and confidence as it has with me, I cannot bear the thought of that, No body deserves this torture inside your head that you can't escape or it appears that way often! I have since learnt with help it can't be escaped from, you have to face it but you can recover and be happier!

Well it's been a few weeks since incident with Damien and my mum and boy do I know about it, she's rang me daily telling me about how shockingly bad Damien is acting and how she can't cope, Only advice I can give her is you need to report this to the police or his key worker or something mum, he doesn't wish to see me, you won't let me near him so what really apart from support you can I do?

Today my mum told me Damien was still at it with his bad behaviour and wasn't listening to anyone at all as he'd only gone and called the dinner lady at school a fat cow! Honestly, I am wondering will he ever learn any respect for himself and others, will anything scare him to do so? Upon the head of year hearing this obviously she called him to her office, she later reported to my mum that he sat with an attitude on him and said he doesn't care said she was an idiot so why should he listen to her, when my mum got home and asked him why he had acted that way yet again he said 'she is an idiot so I am only telling truth it is how I feel' and he shrugged his shoulders, Damien then went on to say to my mum, 'I do not care for her or anyone only for myself' and he then refused to leave his room but not before telling my mum to 'get out as she will be dead in 3 weeks' time and joining her brother soon!'

Damien isn't supposed to leave mums yard without one of his older siblings with him, this often fell to Katie as she was the only one my mum deemed maturely responsible enough to watch him but again only a few days after the school incident he told my mum to go away not so politely and walked out her yard and up the lane by himself, My mum then went on to say how she wished it was just that one thing but also Rory has decided to also act up and had attempted to drive the mule at the livery yard that the people there use to clean the school and stables out and Rory had managed to damage it somehow at the cost of £270 to my mum plus another £380 she had to find for steering column for my mum's mobility car she had not long bought under the right to buy under the mobility scheme he also tried to take my mums car that night and had broken the key in the steering lock breaking the ignition barrel meaning my mum now needed a new car as there was other stuff the car needed that at time wasn't too bad but total it all up my mum just didn't have much option but to consider having to get another mobility car.

Throughout all of this I'm stressed to max with concern thinking how bad my kids must feeling to be acting out like this, to me I saw it as my kids crying out for help as I once did, I was also deeply concerned by my mums recent behaviour and really am worried for her mental wellbeing, you see she's telling anyone that'll listen including me that my uncle Edward isn't dead (she can't accept it even though it has been 2 years now) and she is telling people that he is on his Jols (my mums word for Holidays) that he is currently in Australia and that he's travelling the world like he has always wanted to do, but he's had to stop for a little bit longer than planned in the out backs of Australia which has delayed him and since he is in the out backs he can't get in touch as there is no signal, he's there as he went snorkelling with a leggy blonde bit and a shark bit his toe and even though he is ok, he's obviously needing to rest and that is why no one has heard nor seen from him but he's perfectly ok! When anyone tries speaking to her about this has I have tried a few times, she says yes I know but I can't accept it nor wish to so please leave it I can't deal with it, I need to do it this way so just do not say he's in well there has no he isn't please ok love! So what can we do?

Over the next few week's things again for no reason become strained between me and my mum contact just slowed right down, even the texts which used be non-stop all day on wattapp have now dwindled down to one a day if that I can only imagine it is because I told my mum how worried I was and begged her to at least go Drs or speak to someone professionally as she needs to grieve that was the last meaningful time she really tried with me since, I guess truth does hurt

Only a few weeks after me telling me mum this, I was visiting my nanna in Stanford, I was just leaving and had got into my car when my mum turned up as me and nanna had left hers and was walking to my car when we noticed my mums car was parked beside my car, knowing she wasn't speaking I said Hi then got straight into my car, My mum at this point knocked on my car window, I put my window down and she said to me 'you have a flat tyre' I thought she was trying to get me out the car playing one her usual not funny jokes as per usual as it wasn't unusual for her to say something for you to then look and her laugh and think she was hilarious and say something dumb, so I just said yeah right whatever and I carried on home and by time I had driven the 9 miles home I had forgot all about it as the driving did feel weird but nothing too major and once home I simply forgot to look at it until 2 days later when me and James went out to use the car and James noticed the tyre was indeed flat and suddenly I thought back to what my mum had said and looked at my tyre more closely..... There was a slash mark on the wall of my tyre....surely not?

RISE OF DAMIEN!

Well, this IS definitely the rise of Damien …..Hell on earth has officially started I am afraid to say hahaha! In July 2018 my youngest son Damien ran away from my mum's after yet another of their many recent arguments…… She rang me a good few hours after he had ran away, It was 9pm when my mum rang me to say what had happened, he had gone off on one again as he was late home from school and had got himself told off for it as usual and gone to his room as he always did and my mum thought no more of it until she shouted him through hours later for his tea but instead of Damien staying in his room reading or writing as he usually did, he had on this day climbed out of his bedroom window and ran away, my mum was to be fair very frantic with worry and angry and emotional as was I and I told my mum I was coming through!

James drove me through to my mum's to go pick her and Dean up so we could go out in my car and search the surrounding areas for Damien as up to now all my mum had done was ring the police to report him missing who now had patrol cars out looking for him too, we searched everywhere for hours upon hours, all the villages that surrounded my mum's area there was Hackfield, Dancraft, Stanford, Thinkle just to name a few in walking distance around my mums and since he had no money that we knew of we presumed he had to be on foot, we also searched the disused golf course and all its creepy out buildings that was pitch black by this time and quite eerie to be creeping around in, we walked to the railway lines and checked on there, all the local parks, drove up and down the streets, shouting his name, I and Dean got out and walked the streets asking people if they had seen him and giving them a description and showing a photo, all of them said No, It felt hopeless and even though we didn't want to we had to give up looking at 2 am and go home, what more could we do but in these hours out looking I had noticed to say the police had informed my mum patrol cars was out looking we didn't spot 1 police vehicle at all in all the time we was out looking for Damien!

I went home and logged onto my Facebook account and created a post that went something like "Missing Damien, Aged 15 vulnerable natured, not street wise, being missing all evening now, Police are aware and looking, please contact me if spotted, Thank you" and I attached a photo of Damien and I posted it in all the local groups and asked everyone to please share!

By 11 am I had a message! Damien was safe and at a ladies in Hackfield, I flew through their in my car whilst I was trying to ring my mum I must have tried 5 times and each time there was no answer, I rang my nanna spoke to my cousin Candy who said she'd ring my mum…. A half-hour later my mum rings says she is parked up outside at dawns the ladies will I let her in so Dawn goes to do so but I had been their 20 minutes by now, It was my first time seeing my son in 9 years never mind all ALONE! Well, apart from dawn but hey I am still in tears! I ask him why he had ran away and that I was not mad but needed to know so I could help him and he says I'm not happy mum, he then tells me he was never asked if he wanted to see me at any point by any one whilst he had been with my mum, says he knew nothing about courts etc.? He thought I'd dumped him, they'd told him he was just going on holiday to nanna's then left him there with no further explanation and he didn't understand, he hugged me, I hugged him and we both cried he said he wanted to come home, to give me a second chance, I told him about James etc. and he nodded said yes! I told him it'd not be so easy and they would need a lot doing paperwork, social services possible it'd have to also go through the courts and could take time and he'd have to also tell social workers and school etc. and police his wishes too and he said yes anything it takes, but what about nanna, I do not want to upset her and she will not like it, I said it does not matter, you matter, your happiness and nanna will come around eventually, she loves you and was worried last night and yes she would miss you, but she wants you happy too.

My mum arrived in the kitchen said Hi and I told her what Damien had just said to me and he confirmed it to my mum, she then took Damien home and I went my nanna's after thanking Dawn and informed her what had just happened, my whole family said by the time she rings you Damien will have changed his mind as Jossalynn will have made him!   I thought no chance.....they know my mum well! She rang and informed me Damien had decided he now wanted to see me but not move in!   A few weeks later Damien decides actually yes he does want move in and he's telling everyone it's happening before it even is, we agree he can stay overnight one day a week on a Saturday night to see how it goes and to help him transition and make it easier for us all plus I had nothing at this point in form of bedroom items for him apart from a bed I had kindly being given, this happened Damien staying over around 3 times then It suddenly without any real planning just jumped to Fri and sat night's I admit I was ecstatic and I wasn't seeing how rushed this was, how quickly my mum was pushing it all, How disastrous this could be, all I could see was my son wanted us to be a family and I wanted to be his mum!

By Xmas 2018 Damien had all but officially fully moved in he had a room, a bed and TV, Xbox for Xmas and after Xmas he never really left our home and me and James were asked to attend a parenting course we agreed to do a Triple P parenting programme for troubled teenagers and got a certificate in it!

Whoop We was now fully qualified parent's and held certificates to say so too, so there you go kids do not come with manuals but you can get a certificate in parenting skills hahaha!

Well I'd love to say all was great and we was all this big happy family and how perfect it all was and to be fair for a while it really was, we had days out to Bridlington, Lincoln Castle, Theme parks you name it we all went to it, but James was seeing something I wasn't or didn't want too, a darker side to Damien that wasn't so nice, a vindictive side James tried sitting me down and telling me but I didn't/wasn't hearing any of it.

A few months after Christmas I think it was March me and James decided to go to London for Day to a Brexit event which was sooo awesome to be part of and we really enjoyed it, It was the break we needed and the people I met there was to become a huge support in my life and also a pain in many ways too, it was a great time and when we got back later that day Damien was ok, had said he had a good day and enjoyed the trust of being at home himself and felt grown up so In May 2019 we decided as Damien was 16 we would go away for 1 night to London to a Veterans Event for a protest against Historical crimes being brought against our veterans in the UK as coming from Military families ourselves we both supported this whole heartedly as could easily be any of our family members being charged next, It was an amazing event and we met some truly amazing people who I am proud to call lifelong friends, We had originally planned to send Damien and 1 of his friends on a camping trip for his 16th birthday celebrations while we went to London but his behaviour had been that bad we felt treating him to that degree would be irresponsible of us so we decided that he was possibly responsible enough to stay at home overnight alone, we quickly learnt we was wrong their too and this was a bad judgement on our side as upon our arrival home we were greeted with a bit of a mess!

Alvin our dog was trapped in the living room when before we went away we made it clear to Damien please do not leave the dog in the room alone, also our front door was unlocked and Damien was out! He had gone school leaving the door unlocked and dog trapped in living room there was dog poo and urine everywhere it stank! Thanks, Damien one job mate, Kitchen was a mess food everywhere, dirty pots in the sink not on the side as we had shown him to stack them or even better why not washed? Spilt milk on the sofa and it was left to dry as a white stain and smelt sour....Honestly the list just goes on but worse still, I'd noticed a few pieces of my jewellery missing from my bedroom out my jewellery box I don't own much so it was easily spotted and some money around £85 I had in another handbag saved up! I ask Damien about this upon him coming home from school and his reply was oh shit! I don't know why I did that with the dog or the door but I was rushing as was late up and was late for bus to get to school on time but other wasn't me, I did not take anything so I don't know....anyone been in then such as a mate or owt... he simply replies...No?

So how Damien did this happen.... How did my earrings break were has 2 pairs gone too, were did the money go huh? I don't know was his reply, it wasn't me, followed by tears. He goes to his room, I'm lost for words and also in tears as I know he is lying to me, I can see it in his eyes, I always knew when my children were fibbing to me, I do not know how but I did and unfortunately I knew he was responsible so I and James talk for a good while and together we decide it's best to move forward and hope it's an attention thing and we learnt to ignore negative behaviour on the triple P course and we was to reinforce the good behaviour, so we decided to ground him, stop his pocket money and restrict his Xbox for 1 week.

We had a good few weeks after that but then one day the school rang me Damien had decided to scare the younger children aged 11 and 12 years old with a picture on his phone off mono! (freaky looking stupid craze kids using to scare other kids with serious consequences which have led to kids killing themselves or hurting others) horrible thing to do and I'm fuming! I inform school Damien will lose his phone for a week for this and he does! Not impressed I put restrictions on everything parental controls upon the phone, Xbox, internet everything and I got much stricter too with its use, limited time to 3 hours a day etc.!

Nothing worked his behaviour continued and this put stress on my relationship with James who was starting to resent Damien and James was becoming depressed and very withdrawn, It wasn't fair on any of us, My weight was dropping off me I only weighed 6 stone, I was catching virus after virus and was very fatigued and my fibromyalgia really did play up, I was in agony and the extra work load on James was taking its toll, we was at serious risk of splitting up, things had sunk that low within the household, yet the more me and James argued and drifted apart the happier Damien seemed to become, also I noticed Damien was asking about my health a lot and when I replied I was ok he was moody yet when I stated I was feeling in lots of pain and feeling very weak he got so happy and used to sing and dance around the house, I still aint worked that out yet?

Damien was by this point having no pocket money, wasn't going out, did not go on his Xbox as he had no Xbox live to play his favourite game which he spent most of his time playing called was fornite but this did not work without a subscription to Xbox live, Damien was just sat in our living room or his bedroom when he wasn't at school, I encouraged him to go to the cadets and local youth club on our estate to meet new friends, we managed to get him to agree to go to army cadets closer to home as one he attended was such a distant and he went youth club once a week and things picked up a little and we thought we would again test him out and planned another trip to London and when we got back from London that second time and Damien again decided he was this time going to steal more money from us plus a pair of my diamond earrings, my husband's late father's military items that he used to collect before he passed only in Dec 2018 being a veteran himself he loved collecting cap badges and he loved them dearly so obviously they meant a lot to my hubby too!

We hit the roof and James stated I am sorry but if he was my kid I'd have hit him before now, James was stood in our hallway at Damien's door, I was beside of James also in doorway just in front of James and I placed my hand on James chest and calmly I told James to take Alvin around block to calm down while I speak to Damien please and James did so, I spoke to Damien in quite a stern voice and I told him he would not be trusted again now and he would have to earn that trust back which would take a long time and a lot of hard work on his side to now do if he wanted any trust from us and that we had spoken and agreed that we wanted his house key back as when we were not in the house Damien wasn't to be either, I wasn't going to have any further items stolen enough was enough, I decided not go police as he was my son and he wanted to go into army and with his past record stabbing my mum I didn't wish to be the reason his career was ruined. He cried and said sorry, I went into room and more softly said sorry is a word Damien and one that comes very easily to you, actions speak louder and now it is time for actions so give me your house key please, to which Damien gave me his key and James returned home and me and James went into the living room, I explained what had just been said between Damien and I and James agreed with me that once Damien had done his exams at school if his behaviour had not improved that he should move into a youth hostel as Damien cannot follow even the simplest of instructions and certainly doesn't follow order or rules and since my weight was now dangerously low and I was still losing weight and Drs didn't know why along with other symptoms, I knew if I didn't put myself and my health first I would be dead within a year I honestly felt that weak.

It was to be either Damien in a Hostel or similar place, me dead or me and James splitting up and apart from troubles with Damien we were otherwise very happy so splitting up made very little sense to me, Damien was 16, he was going into the Army he'd already said that at 17 or 18 he was going into Harrogate then into Army, so I'd chuck my 9yr relationship away for nothing when we still loved each other very much, No that made no sense at all, No that certainly was not happening, no questions or thoughts needed on that topic, James had been there for me throughout all this, throughout all my tears he had picked me up I wasn't walking away now, we went in this together and we would come out of it together. So I decide to tell Damien that he even improved his behaviour and remained with us, supporting him and helping him or he carried on this path to destruction and we would have no option but to help him obtain a room in a youth hostel but before I can do so my phone bleeps, a text from my mum... She is setting off in 5 minutes and will be on her way to collect Damien so make sure he's all packed I said what and she says has he told me and that is ok yes? I replied Told me what mum I aint amused? Her reply was simply ring me to which I obviously do so and she says, 'I have just got off phone with Damien and he has asked to come back to live here love with me, he said you was ok with it', I said I was not aware of this but I replied 'Yes that is ok if it is what he wants', I come off phone and turn and tell James my mum is on her way to collect Damien as it turns out Damien wants to go back to live with my mum to which James replies well that makes things easier and your mum is ok with him after last time?

I go through to Damien's bedroom to ask him and he has already almost packed all his belongings and clothing up and is not crying at all and states it's not working out so he's going back my mums until after his exams and he is going into YMCA to live by himself and be his own boss as he is perfectly fine without any of us, which fetches us to current day and is currently where he is living now in the YMCA he is claiming Universal Credit each month and he is attending a local army college which he gets a bursary for attending each week too so is easily on over £450 a month in total he gets plus he gets his rent paid too, he should for 16 years old be living a pretty dam good life, but he is useless with money and as usual still not listening and instead each month he withdraws his money and blows the lot of it, one time was a iPad, following time was a new phone, his clothes are too small yet he won't buy new, he is missing out on trips and activities in his college and cadets as he is wasting his money instead of being sensible paying his mates to run his YouTube channel etc., you see at moment Damien isn't speaking to me again but it does not mean when I hear these things I do not worry or stress at how he is ruining his life, never has any food etc. as he is wasting money on daft things yet even though he has learnt what being without food feels like he still has not learnt his lesson, I just prey he realises soon.

THE FUTURE

It's currently 1 week before Christmas in 2019 and I have finally written this book! It has only taken me 8 years to do in total, It's been a painful book to write, I've left it mostly unedited in the style of how I speak imagine me reading it to you in a South Yorkshire accent hahaha, The book style is in a sort of a journal, diary and biography all in one based upon life, my emotional journey through the darkness, the laughter, the light and everything in-between with all character names and most places changed to protect anyone involved and parts dramatized but I will admit not much of it at all is fiction though I so wish it was.

As it stands with my life at moment, I am 37 years old, Live on a council estate in a 2 bedroom flat ground floor am still extremely underweight at only just 6 stone a size 6 clothing hangs off me! I have fibromyalgia, Joint Hypermobility Syndrome, GERD just to name a few, I'm currently under Dr's care for unexplained weight loss, I weigh 6 stone as I write this and am 5ft 5" so look and feel terribly ill and I feel it too, I have had appointment at hospital awaiting results for that to see why I am losing weight, I am also awaiting tests to see if I have hypermobile Ehlers danlos syndrome or not (hopefully not) but I have an awful lot of the symptoms, unfortunately.

I and James have been together for 10 years on the 28th Jan 2020! We are stronger than we have ever been and very happy and are considering if to move or not in the future (if we haven't done so by this time) we are hoping for a country retreat if we do or anywhere with a garden a nice cottage or bungalow maybe, obviously given we are poor it won't be anywhere flash hahaha but you know what I just want a garden to relax in nothing else matters (well apart from Brexit thanks for that Mr PM)

◆ ◆ ◆

This almost fetches me to an end but an update on how my life is at the moment:

My Children (apart from Damien) still all refuse to acknowledge my existence which is very difficult to cope with and affects my mental health very badly and that alone in return affects my physical conditions, Damien recently informed me after again stealing 80p, yes I was daft and loaned him 80p till later that day thinking he'd pay me back, he choose not to instead he went for food to KFC and cinema with his mate. upon me texting him to ask him about this, he replied he lives alone, doesn't need me, that I had failed him again and that I was worthless and a slag who choose a man over her son and he'd only wanted to split me and James up and hurt me as I'd hurt him as a kid and that I was a drug user and a skank, I admit I smoke cannabis I do not hide that fact I never have, I informed Damien before he moved in and always made no secret of it as it's not for recreational use its 1 medication that is herbal and works without it I am in agony, I can't walk more than a few steps without crying in pain and feeling like I just want life to end, but smoking it I feel happier, less stressed, pain is greatly reduced, I can walk around a supermarket YES in pain but I can do it I can't without it so how can this be a bad thing, I don't steal, I pay my bills, I have food etc. I don't see it as a crime as the police know as do all that are I y life or been in my life, I honestly think it should be legal but I aint saying try it as if you're on medication this could be dangerous plus it does not agree with everyone and can cause serious effects on some people plus addiction issues and other unfortunate effects if misused or if you do not understand it and get given bad stuff, anyhow Damien sent me a text stating all this and wouldn't accept my calls and then said he was done with me, I'd failed him, Goodbye, So I wasn't going to argue, I simply put I'd be here for him when he realises that he has acted wrongly and that he has to apologise for his behaviour and is in the wrong as he can't keep acting like this so goodbye xx

I honestly thought I'd regret sending it but how much can I keep giving and giving and getting hurt?

I'm going to be dead if I keep trying/living this life something has to give, I am currently around 6 stone and I can't eat well nor sleep well, my health is failing me big style, My PTSD is very bad writing this opened new wounds I am on waiting list for rape and sexual assault counselling to once and for all close and fully heal those old wounds but waiting list is 6 months, this really is ridiculous as it isn't just affecting me it is affecting James too and I am offered no support at all in any other form from NHS or otherwise in this 6 months which I find quite shocking, James bless him he has had to go through this all these years, see my health fail and to see me unable to eat through stress yet unable to do anything to actually help me, he tries and succeeds to make me laugh and each day makes me smile, he's my rock without him I would no doubt be dead as life is hard but you know what I have come this far, I will finish this book and I will tell my story and set record straight once and for all and hopefully show my kids the truth and everyone who has wronged me in my life at the hands of my mums vile lies, I do not blame you at all, I understand now how my mum somehow manages to let people see one persona but actually isn't that person at all and when people realise this my mum simply ups and moves and starts life a fresh so she never truly gets found out, yet I keep having the guilt to carry, the stares still continue in the area I live and my kids still do not know the truth, my life isn't perfect far from it, but I've come to learn lots are wrong with this country we live in called UK the government system has failed me on so many levels and along my journey I have learnt it's failed many thousands of others too, from the Law system to the NHS to our education it's all flawed, It needs a fresh total overhaul, also I've learnt not to be ashamed, our government tells us we lose our children for a reason but sad fact is as I have proven this is not always the case, sexual cases, mental breakdowns, false allegations, pain, misery, losing your children because of what could happen not because of what has happened known as crystal ball method and is based on the likelihood of things happening rather than using facts which you'd not treat anyone guilty of a crime this way the crown prosecution would not charge me for an incident that aint happened so how can the law act lawfully in these cases? ....all this IS and does happen and sad fact is it is possibly happening to someone you know right now, maybe it is you? Maybe you just suspect....whichever it is... Please don't just do nothing, I did out of shame for many years and I now know I have nothing at all to be ashamed of at all and in fact, I have a lot to hold my head up high for. I am intelligent, I am honest and I don't hide behind any smokescreen, I smoke weed for pain relief and I don't believe in acts of parliament, I am a rebel with a cause, I am a patriot, a survivor.... I'm getting stronger and slowly gaining in confidence too and even though at times I struggle through each day I am proof life IS worth carrying on when it is at its darkest I am that light! If I can do it you can too, I am no different at all from you, I aint strong, I certainly am not brave and I would not say I am fully recovered not at all I am still recovering and my journey on this emotional rollercoaster aint yet come to an end, the ride I am sure still has lots more twists and turns and possible dark tunnels along the way too but the darkness has faded once and it will again and the light is becoming much brighter and for longer each time.

◆ ◆ ◆

I am now a Nanna! my daughter Katie gave birth to a beautiful little girl in December, congratulations Katie, I have unfortunately only seen three photographs of my Granddaughter Rose-Louise as Katie has made it clear I will NEVER be a nanna to her and will never get to hold my beautiful granddaughter or see her nor am I able to buy my granddaughter anything, she is the double of her mummy though, so I am currently riding a whole new level of pain, It's December 29th me and James did not celebrate Christmas this year, it is always just the two of us anyhow we never get invited anywhere, neither us now have family, both us are struggling as it is a year since my husband lost his dad and for me it doesn't feel right celebrating when it's my granddaughters first Christmas and I asked my mum if I can at least buy a present for Christmas my mum said she would ask my daughter, later that day my mum texted me back to say that my daughter told my mum No she will not accept anything from me, so as it stands right now my mum knows about me writing this book though I don't think she actually believes me nor thinks I am capable of writing and getting a book published she must still think I am way too stupid for that, so she thinks I'm living in cloud cuckoo land, oupsie mum but I did try to warn you and even sent you the book cover and explained you would not like it, I actually hoped to sit and go through it and put your views into it but you made it clear you don't think it'll happen but wish me good luck anyhow.

Over the Christmas period my youngest son Damien had texted me and we spoke and agreed to a fresh start, James too agreed in time he too would be willing to give Damien another chance which to me was better than any present I could have wished for, I just hope and pray that this is for real as with my past, with what Damien himself told me and my mum has told me over the years she's took great pleasure in multiple times informing me that Damien has told her and Katie and anyone else who will listen that he has only moved in with me when he did to hurt me and cause me as much pain as possible and after Damien telling me as much in that text a few weeks ago it has made me feel doubtful but he is my son and I love him dearly and wish so much for us to have a proper Mother & Son relationship, It is all I wish for all my children & myself is for us to be at least on speaking terms, letting me in their life's and seeing I really am not that monster I am painted out to be, In fact I am human, I make mistakes, I act daft and I never take myself seriously or life seriously, I am I think good fun but most of all I understand what you my precious children have been through as I too have been through it too, so I can help you more than you realise, I am sorry if you are reading this and the truth hurts, It never has been nor will ever be my intention to hurt any of you, I love you more than I could ever express into words, I miss you and hope one day you read this and realise you are not alone, you are each beautiful in your own way and you each have your own talents and skills...You are each beautiful inside and out, In fact that goes for any of you reading this book you are all beautiful in your own rights!

I can be found on Facebook search for Emma Cruize Emotional Roller-coaster to join my page and I promise to respond to each comment personally and support you to best I am able to do so, You are not alone together we can heal but for now much love always and safe travels. Over next few pages I have spent some time putting together a few bits of information on Narcissistic Personality Disorder, PTSD and helpful websites and such forth I hope they start to help you like they did me.

God Bless!

Much Love

Emma xx

NARCISSISTIC PERSONALITY DISORDER

WHAT IS A NARCISSISTIC?

N arcissistic people's objective in life is simply to destroy the victim, the narcissist uses the following control tactics to manipulate and deceive their victim:

- Gaslighting; this is when the abuser creates a scenario where the victim questions their reality and what has happened. After time and repetition, the victim becomes confused and may feel they are going insane.

- Projection; the narcissist blames you for their bad behaviour. They project and accuse you of behaviour, they are in fact doing themselves.

- Circular conversations; Conversations with a narcissist will include changing the subject, false accusatory statements to shift the blame and focus of the conversations, and to side rail and cause confusion. Nothing gets resolved.

- Invalidation; The narcissist will create an environment where thoughts or feelings are not responded to appropriately to create a sense of inferiority, not being heard or understood, and not validated or supported. The individual is made to feel less than and not good enough.

- Personal Jokes; they may joke and with a dig regarding your personality or situation and then claim they were just kidding and to not take it so seriously.

- Smear campaigns; a narcissist will launch false information to friends and family. These campaigns may consist of 5% truth, and 95% lies. These smear campaigns and are told in a way that the audience will believe the narcissist.

- False Accusation; The narcissistic abuser will constantly make false accusatory statements. The victim oftentimes feels the need to defend, which gives the narcissist the supply they needed which is Lies, Lies and more Lies. They will tell you lies, and when they are caught in a lie, they simply use deniability.

- Blame shifting; a narcissist fails to take responsibility for their actions or inactions. It's always someone else's fault.

- Baiting; a narcissist will set up a scenario where the victim is known to react with anger, or hostility

- Isolation; the narcissist will try to cause an interruption with established relationships.

- Embarrassment; the narcissist will often choose to embarrass you in public or at special occasions.

- Constant High Level of Criticism; a narcissist's criticism can be over anything at any time. This sends a signal to their victim they are not good enough, not capable so the victim tries harder to please and perform. When the victim performs well, it is never acknowledged, and the carrot is moved to never reach the goal so to speak.

- Emotional Abuse; emotional abuse comes in many forms, the narcissist will belittle, berate, discredit, ignore, undermine and devalue. The victim feels afraid and unable to be whom they are.

- Silent treatment; they will ignore your needs and show lack of empathy toward your distresses.

- Through her behaviour, you begin to realize that she could blow up at anything you do, which can lead to you feeling like you can never do anything right. It is likely that through her words she also reinforces the belief that you are bad at everything, making you truly believe that you are incapable.

The narcissist will try to abuse and take advantage of your good traits and try to destroy and tear you down. You may feel shame to keep your past covered but I encourage you to speak out and share your truth and learn to be a voice of compassion and victory for others who have also been abused, Shame will keep you silent but you have nothing what so ever to feel guilt or shame about...Please remember that always!

Your Perception of Reality is not true a big and often dangerous belief system that victims of narcissistic parents grow up with is that their perception of reality is not true. This mistrust in their perception of reality leads to the belief that they are incapable of recalling events as they happened, and it is caused by narcissistic people lying to others and to their children to cover up their abuse. This chronic lying and twisting of events can make it feel like you are incapable of remembering anything factually, which leaves you believing that you have to rely on others to recount facts for you because you are incapable. This can be particularly dangerous as it can completely distort your sense of reality and leave you trusting in the wrong people to provide you with a true sense of reality, the truth of the matter is, the only positive way to work through this belief system is to reinforce trust in yourself and learn to believe in your perception of reality. It is never a good or safe idea to place this amount of trust and task outside of yourself as it will leave you vulnerable to abuse while also keeping your sense of self-esteem, self-confidence, and self-trust low.

How does a narcissistic/abusive mother or father behave?

Here are some of the main signs:

- They tried to control you through co-dependency
- They laid on the guilt thick
- They only loved you when you did what THEY wanted
- They liked to "get even" with you
- They never respected your boundaries
- They competed with you
- They "owned" your accomplishments
- They constantly lied to you
- They never listened to (or cared) about your feelings
- They constantly insulted you
- They exerted explicit control over you
- They gaslighted you
- They "parentified" you
- They had a "favourite" or "golden" child
- They reacted intensely to any form of criticism
- They projected their bad behaviour onto you

- They never displayed any empathy
- They were infallibly correct and never wrong
- They liked to present a perfect family image to outsiders
- One of their favourite lines is; I've done so much for you, I've sacrificed everything for you!

If you're the child of a narcissist, you will likely struggle with these problems:

- Co-dependency in other relationships
- Weak sense of self, never good enough or valuable enough
- Poor personal boundaries and inability to say "no"
- Chronic guilt or toxic shame
- Self-loathing
- Emptiness
- Trust issues
- Inability to express or handle emotions (resulting in emotional numbness)
- Anxiety or depression
- Being a people-pleaser
- Very attuned (to an almost uncanny degree) to what everyone around them is feeling, because they have a hyper-sensitivity to what others are experiencing
- Chronically unsure of themselves, and overly-worried about what others think of them

The hypnotic hold a narcissistic mother has on her daughter can be so strong and pathological that the child doesn't know what she is thinking or feeling.

To outsiders, your parent is a larger-than-life social magnet who attracts people from all walks of life but behind closed doors, all pretence falls away, only you, their child knows what it's really like to endure their cold shoulders for days on end over a minor infraction, or to bear the brunt of constant, age-inappropriate demands for perfection and strength, you know what it's like to be parented by a narcissist, you didn't imagine any of it, this did happen.

I've found too that narcissistic parents demand that you agree with them or else they'll reject you, because being challenged to them means they are not loved.

Healing from narcissistic abuse

• Educate Yourself about Narcissism as the more you educate yourself and find support, the more you will understand what you've been through and what you need to do to move beyond the toxic influence of your family.

• Accept That Your Narcissist Parent Won't Change by holding out hope that your parent will finally give you the unconditional love you have craved your whole life is natural, but it is a false dream that makes you vulnerable to further abuse and keeps you from moving on.

• Assert Boundaries one of the most difficult and important things you must do for yourself as a survivor is to establish healthy boundaries.

• Attune with Your Feelings you have been systematically trained to ignore your feelings, even to fear and hate them. Try not to judge yourself. Feelings are feelings are feelings. They deserve, and in the scheme of things insist upon, recognition and respect.

• Don't Blame yourself you are likely to automatically blame yourself and feel guilt for things beyond your control or responsibility. Narcissists are experts at deflecting and projecting blame onto others. If they raged at you and you stood up for yourself, you attacked them. If they punched you, you drove them to it. One of the best ways to break your unhealthy family dynamics is to stop blaming yourself for what was never your responsibility or fault to begin with.

• Stop Hurting Yourself As someone raised in a narcissistic family, you are prone to risky, self-punishing, and self-soothing but destructive behaviours, such as substance abuse and addictions, self-harm, and thrill-seeking. Your self-destructive behaviour is an internalization of the narcissistic abuse you grew up with, seek help and support from people who understand the dynamics of Narcissism I have put links I found useful on links to support I found helpful page of this book.

• Honour Your Feelings about Your Narcissist Parent Most of us love our parents, no matter what, and we cling to our need for love and validation from them. Your narcissistic parent cannot love you unconditionally the way we all deserve to be loved within our families, and for that matter is capable of no more than fleeting empathy. Yet you may still love that parent. Mixed with grief and anger, you may also sympathize with your parent's NPD. It is also possible that you are numb to your parent or too used up to feel love anymore, whatever your feelings are don't be told by anyone you shouldn't feel that way, don't allow judgement accept its your feelings and you are entitled to feel that way. Narcissist parents, unless they are true sadists, are usually capable of affection for their children, at least sometimes. Some may be able to give in ways that you find nurturing or helpful. With a healthy dose of scepticism, take the good when it comes, as limited as it may be.

If you are dealing with the effects of growing up in a dysfunctional family please, find a support group to attend in your area. If you need more extensive help, the people in those support groups will help you find professionals in the area that can treat your issues.

Help is available to everyone, but you need to reach out and ask for it. I know because I have done it, and I am just like you.

You don't have to live your life feeling depressed, unworthy, or dependent on unhealthy coping mechanisms, such as drugs, alcohol, or food, which will only temporarily numb your pain. You don't need to spend the rest of your days following the trajectory chosen for you when someone else took away your innocence.

It is possible to reclaim who you could have been, but you have to first acknowledge that you were a victim, confront the pain and the shame, and let other people in so they can help.

Are you willing to reach out for help so you can take your life back?

Post-traumatic stress disorder (PTSD) afflicts some people who have undergone a traumatic event involving serious injury or a threat to life or limb. Initially identified in combat veterans, PTSD seems to result as well from natural disasters, child abuse, and other devastating experiences. People with PTSD keep re-experiencing the traumatic event in waking life or in dreams, and they actively avoid situations that might bring back memories of the trauma. They may also suffer a general numbing of their responsiveness, show diminished interest in significant activities, restrict the range of their emotions, or have feelings of detachment or estrangement from others. Finally, they may also experience increased arousal (such as difficulty falling or staying asleep), irritability or outbursts of anger, difficulty concentrating, hyper vigilance, and an exaggerated startle response.

HOW CHILD ABUSE AFFECTS
ADULT SURVIVORS

For those who mistakenly believe that the damaging effects of child abuse are outgrown by childhood this information may come as a painful surprise. The fact is that the effects of child abuse last into adulthood and throughout one's life. Its effects are often deleterious, meaning that the impact is often delayed and slow to develop but acute when they do occur. The consequence is that many adults who were abused during childhood experience its worst effects long after they have entered adulthood.

The experiences of child abuse can stay with survivors for a long time. Adults who have buried their history of child abuse can continue to suffer in ways that can include post-traumatic stress disorder (PTSD), eating disorders, substance misuse, depression, anxiety, low self-esteem, anger, guilt, learning disabilities, physical illness, disturbing memories and dissociation. One particular issue is the challenge of forming and keeping adult relationships.

Child abuse can adversely affect the development of the personality of the survivor and their ability to regulate their emotions, which can lead to self-destructive and impulsive behaviour, such as repeated self-harm or recurrent suicide attempts. Those who have been repeatedly abused over time can suffer dissociation and go into trance-like states, often triggered by reminders of the abuse, in which they relive abusive experiences.

*Symptoms experienced mostly by
those who were abused by children:*

1. Lack of trust in other people. Sometimes this distrust can resemble paranoia.

2. Chronic feelings and thoughts of guilt about anything and everything that happens to them and to others.

3. A tendency to choose partners who continue the abusive behaviours they experienced during their childhood. Some of these people do become abusive but, most often they continue to re-experience abuse in their lives.

4. A fear that underneath, they are just like the abusive parent and that, therefore, they are inherently evil or are a "bad seed."

5. These feelings and thoughts are tenacious and are resistant to anyone giving this person any kind of compliment.

6. Even when these patients learn that they were abused at the hands of one or both parents, there is a continued tendency to explain away parental abusive as having been deserved.

7. Low self-esteem.

8. Chronic, low level depression.

9. Generalized anxiety caused by no particular event in the present.

10. Panic attacks usually associated with post-traumatic stress disorder (PTSD).

11. Social isolation due to a lack of friendships.

12. Conflicted and difficult marriages.

13. Dissociative disorders in which the survivor of child abuse goes into a "fugue" state in which they are unaware of what they are doing or where they have been. It is a defence against stress

which, when it happens, brings the person back to the original childhood trauma.

14. Most of the other symptoms associated with depression and anxiety.

For more information on how the effects of childhood abuse can affect your brain etc. please take a read at this interesting website; https://www.dana.org/article/wounds-that-time-wont-heal/

Also If you suspect a child is being abused or you require more information this website is amazing; https://www.nspcc.org.uk/what-is-child-abuse/types-of-abuse/neglect/

Another great website is survivors.org they are for MALE rape and sexual abuse survivors https://www.survivorsuk.org/question/grooming/

Lastly another great site is; https://www.helpguide.org/

What help is available?

Shame is a major barrier to survivors seeking help. This is often exacerbated if their appeals for help or disclosure about their abuse as children were ignored or dismissed by family or professionals. Knowing that effective treatment is available is important.

Counselling is a useful starting point and can help survivors by providing a safe environment to develop a trusting therapeutic relationship. It is often the first experience that survivors have of being truly understood in a way that others who haven't been abused are unable to manage. They are heard and believed and experience empathy rather than judgement.

There are self-help resources available also on this website you may find useful along with much more useful info; https://www.safeline.org.uk/resources/

Therapy options;

Cognitive behavioural therapy (CBT) is a fast growing and widely recognised treatment used to help people deal with a variety of psychological difficulties. The evaluation of CBT has shown a 50% success rate in treating anxiety and depression – significantly higher than other talking therapies – and studies have also shown that it can be more effective than medication alone when treating such disorders.

CBT is a structured, action-oriented and problem solving approach which helps people to manage their thoughts, behaviour and mood more effectively. In general, patients will meet with their therapist on a weekly basis for a period of roughly 6-20 sessions which will follow a structured process including the completion of homework and behavioural experiments. CBT has been modified to offer specific help to those suffering from PTSD. It can help survivors process their traumatic experiences in ways that reduce their impact in the present.

Dialectical behaviour therapy (DBT) is a psychological treatment developed for those who experience problems with emotional control after traumatic experiences. It is very focused on teaching skills to improve self-regulation.

Childhood trauma often leads to re-experiencing of painful memories which are difficult to ignore. Eye movement desensitisation and re-processing (EMDR) is a psychological intervention which has been developed to process painful memories. Sessions are sometimes longer than CBT for PTSD, but treatment can be completed in fewer sessions for some cases. Those more severely affected by PTSD may benefit from psychiatric treatment with medication, usually antidepressants.

LINKS TO WEBSITES/ GROUPS & OTHER PLACES TO SEEK SUPPORT I FOUND USEFUL:

• https://www.knightstemplar.org.uk/ these have become my family & good friends, the support from the Facebook page you can join once become a member really has helped me the most, the people are amazing, kind, caring and extremely supportive and free of judgement, this truly is high on my advice of places to go if you care about building loving, loyal friends that will soon become your family and always someone around for support night or day.

KT-UK welcomes new brothers and sisters......
Together we are strong. United. We dont put people down..........we lift them up.

KT-UK

Loyalty, Strength, Honour, Trust & charity.
www.knightstemplar.org.uk

• https://www.womensaid.org.uk/ a grassroots federation working together to provide life-saving services and build a future where domestic violence is not tolerated, the website also has a handbook I found extremely useful and lots of other information.

• https://www.citizensadvice.org.uk/family/gender-violence/domestic-violence-and-abuse-organisations-which-give-information-and-advice/ If you're a victim of domestic violence or abuse, there are many different organisations which can help you and on this page you will find many useful websites.

Printed in Great Britain
by Amazon